ALSO BY ARDEN POWELL

A Summer Soundtrack for Falling in Love

the Faerie Hounds *of* York

Arden Powell

The Faerie Hounds of York
Copyright © 2020 by Arden Powell

This is a work of fiction. Names, characters, places, and incidents either are the product of the author's imagination or are used fictitiously. Any resemblance to actual persons, living or dead, events, or locales is entirely coincidental.

Cover art and book design by Arden Powell.

All rights reserved. No part of this book may be reproduced or transmitted in any form or by any means, electronic or mechanical, including photocopying, recording, or by any information storage and retrieval system without the written permission of the copyright owner, and where permitted by law. Reviewers may quote brief passages in a review.

Autumn prince and hawthorn child,
Fled the heathers and the wild.
Yorkshire born but London raised,
Where went those early boyhood days?
Who buried summer's apples
'neath the bite of winter's frost?
Come back to northern moorland
And regain what has been lost.

TABLE OF CONTENTS

CHAPTER ONE: THE FAERIE RING	11
CHAPTER TWO: THESE RESTLESS DREAMS	34
CHAPTER THREE: THE LOXLEY HOUSE	43
CHAPTER FOUR: ROUGH SLEEP	58
CHAPTER FIVE: GRACE BLACKBURN	72
CHAPTER SIX: THE CHANGELING TEST	90
CHAPTER SEVEN: UNNATURAL ACTS	106
CHAPTER EIGHT: THE HAWTHORN TREE	123
CHAPTER NINE: ROSA'S TALE	139
CHAPTER TEN: THE HOUNDS	152
CHAPTER ELEVEN: THE GRAVE BENEATH THE HAWTHORN	166
CHAPTER TWELVE: THE DOOR TO FAERIE	183
CHAPTER THIRTEEN: THE STRANGER ON THE HILL	193

the Faerie Hounds *of* York

CHAPTER ONE

THE FAERIE RING

Loxley woke cold and stiff. He was not in his bed but on the ground outside, his clothes crisp with frost, and with moss tousled in his hair. His fingers ached, and he unfurled them slowly as he rose to his hands and knees. Hurting all over, his back protested with every movement, and his neck was sore, his coat collar chafing the skin. As if filled with fog, his mind was curiously blank, and his thoughts were slow to return to him.

Something was wrong.

The purple heather was flattened where he had lain; the sky above stretched pale and grey in all directions. It was just past dawn, the November air chill and damp.

But more troubling than his location in the heathered moors was the ring of mushrooms that encircled him where he knelt.

An instinctive fear flared in him at the sight, and his breath stuttered as he froze in his attempt to rise. The mushrooms grew on thick, cream-coloured stalks, their caps broad and brown and speckled with pale teardrop markings. Though they did not form an intimidating physical border, growing only a few inches tall, he did not dare break their circle.

Lowering himself back down, he examined one in closer detail. Wild mushrooms were nothing uncommon, and he had even spotted rings before—they were said to spring up around sources of rot, all superstition aside— but he had never been so foolish as to step into one. They were rarely seen in England; indeed, almost unheard of in his day and age, and it was generally accepted that such old magic had long since returned to its deep slumber beneath the earth.

"I wouldn't touch that, if I were you."

Loxley flinched, twisting around to face the speaker.

A man sat some yards away under a tree beyond the circle's border, a gnarl of roots his throne, with one long leg crossed over the other, a pipe in hand. The tree's leaves were fiery copper, and its canopy was resplendent with a host of bright red apple-like berries, which lay scattered across the ground at the man's feet. It was a hawthorn tree, a sight that tugged at Loxley's foggy memory, and the only one to be seen from one horizon to the other. A faerie tree, he'd heard them called, when they stood alone in a field without another living thing for company. A sign of something old and powerful, best avoided.

The man sitting amongst its roots regarded Loxley with a calm, almost indifferent air, as if he hadn't a care in the world.

"Well, of course I wasn't going to touch it," Loxley said. Whether he believed the old stories or not, he had woken far from home, and the haze in his mind troubled him. Something strange was afoot, and he had no desire to learn firsthand what happened to a soul who broke a faerie ring. "I don't suppose you know how I got here?"

"No, but I can guess." The man took a drag from his pipe; the smoke smelled sweet and spicy.

"Do you know how I might get out again?" Loxley kept his voice purposefully light, to avoid giving strength to his fear. But he could not keep the tremor from his words when he added, "Only, I don't particularly care to be cursed or have my soul stolen away, if I can at all avoid it."

"No," said the man shortly, "you do not."

He tapped the ash from his pipe onto the roots beside him before rising to his feet and approaching the ring. Loxley rose to meet him. Despite the circumstance of their meeting, Loxley was quite certain that the stranger was not, himself, one of the Fair Folk. Though the scent of spiced incense clung to his clothes like magic, his face was too rugged to be anything but human, and his clothes too travel-worn to have any hint of glamour about them. He was of Loxley's height, though broader across the shoulders, and seemed broader still by the cut of his coat. He had brown skin and long, dark hair barely held in check by a tie at the nape of his neck, which made him look to be one of the Romanichal people, though he lacked the bright colours of their dress. Coming to a halt before Loxley and taking care not to step within the circle, he looked Loxley up and down. His eyes were dark as coal, and from Loxley's closer vantage point, now seemed more curious than indifferent.

"You're not from here," he observed.

His accent was thickly northern, his vowels flat and his tone lazily impersonal. He looked Loxley over with a clearly judgemental eye, though whatever opinion he formed, he kept it to himself. His brusqueness seemed born from a lack of regular conversation rather than a dislike of it, and Loxley could forgive a man for that more easily than he could forgive intentional rudeness.

"I was born here," Loxley corrected, faintly, "though I've spent my adult years in London, it's true. I came north because—" There was an uncomfortable gap in his memory where reason ought to have sat. "Where am I, exactly? These are the moors—"

"You're in Yorkshire, and it pays to take more care here."

A shiver ran through Loxley's frame, as if a cool breeze had found its way under his coat to run its fingers down his spine. "Are you talking about magic?" he asked in hushed tones. "But no one has seen one of the Fair Folk in centuries!"

"Not outside of Scotland or Ireland, it's true. Certainly not in London. But man-made borders hold no meaning for the Folk. I've been alive these past four decades and more, yet you've never seen me before today. Did I not exist, either?"

"That's different. I have seen other men, after all. Where are the Fair Folk, if they have been present in England all this time?"

The man shrugged. "I did not say faeries themselves were common, only that their magic has never left the land. I'm no scholar; I can only tell you what I've seen. And I've seen magic. It lingers in the tree roots and the season's first frost. It's deep in the earth—though not so far out of reach as you might think." He bared his teeth in a smile. "This is the north. The land is still half wild up here. It remembers how things used to be."

"You speak of the north as if it were a separate country," Loxley whispered. "We are still in England, are we not?"

"We are. And you're right. No one just wanders into a faerie ring, Londoner or not. You've been played foul, and foulness is clinging to you still."

Loxley's throat was dry, his head throbbing; he must have spent all night on the moors, his head filled with that fog to keep him from waking. But how on earth had he got out there in the first place? It was as if he'd been snatched from his bed: he was still dressed in his nightclothes, under his coat, and his feet were bare in their boots. He swallowed down his fear. There would be time to dwell on such questions later, once he was clear of the danger he had so unwittingly stumbled into. "What foulness?"

"Step out between these two here," the man said, ignoring his query to point to two particular mushrooms at Loxley's feet. They didn't look any different from the others, and Loxley hesitated, torn between the intrinsic fear of breaking the ring and the threat of foul play upon his person. The man rolled his eyes. "Sooner than later, if you please."

Holding his breath, Loxley stepped precisely where the man had pointed, and only exhaled when no gust of wind blew through his body to whisk him away to another world or strike him dead on the spot. Still, there were more insidious ways for Faerie to lay its hooks in a man. Loxley patted himself down, surreptitiously checking that all his limbs were yet accounted for.

"What do you feel?" the man asked, watching him closely.

Aside from a peculiarly sharp sensation in the tip of his right index finger, Loxley felt no different. Upon closer inspection, his fingertip seemed no different, either. It was the place of a sliver of a scar he had borne all his life, and once he rubbed at it, the sharp, prickling feeling dissipated. He pressed his hand over his chest as relief flooded through him, leaving him weak-kneed. "My heart is beating rather fast, but I suppose that's to be expected. How did you do that? What did you do?"

"I broke the enchantment," the man said, as if tampering with faerie magic were something he performed every day. "But only in that precise place, and not for very long. I wouldn't recommend stepping back again." He nodded to the ground behind Loxley's feet, where a new mushroom was poking its tiny cap through the soil to stand between its two brethren where Loxley had passed.

Loxley took a stumbling step away from the ring.

"It was good that you woke when you did; I was considering dragging you out still asleep, and that would have been more dangerous."

"Good," Loxley echoed faintly. "Excellent. Thank you—I suspect I owe you my life." He offered his hand with a shaky smile. "William Loxley, at your service."

"John Thorncress." Thorncress' fingers were long and slender, though his palm was calloused, and his grip was warm and firm. Loxley felt oddly delicate in comparison.

"If there is anything I can do to repay you—" he began, but Thorncress shook his head.

"It was no trouble." He eyed Loxley. "I don't suppose you have any memory of last night, before you came to be here."

"I was—"

In a little room that wasn't his, tossing and turning in the narrow bed, caught halfway between sleep and waking. Memories of tall, dark trees and frost sprites drawing patterns on the windowpane, and a scratching noise against the glass, like something asking to be let inside—

"I must confess, my memory is troublingly unreliable. I think I dreamed of something watching me . . ."

Thorncress lifted his brows.

"But that is silly, of course. I had such dreams often as a child, you see, and for a moment a similar feeling came over me. But that accounts for little."

"Dreams account for more than they are given credit for. But whatever the cause of your misadventure, I advise you return to London as soon as possible. Do you recall where you're staying, at least?"

"I'm afraid not."

Loxley glanced around. The moors stretched endlessly in every direction, broken only by the hawthorn tree, and though the sun was rising above the horizon and lighting up the heather with a delicate hand, it did not seem a safe place to stay for long. The north was not a land where he wished to further lose himself.

"Then I will return you to the place where I'm staying, and you can find your way from there. It wouldn't do to deliver you from one faerie ring just to let you stumble into another."

"I'm quite certain I wouldn't," Loxley began indignantly, but cut himself short when he spotted the slanting smile at the corner of Thorncress' mouth.

"Apologies, sir. I'm certain you do know better than that. Even as a Londoner."

Turning away, Thorncress beckoned to something beyond the tree, and Loxley heard the stamp of hooves before he saw the horse. A great black beast stepped out from behind the trunk, its ears pricked inquisitively, the reins tied back around the saddle to keep them from tangling. It came to a snorting halt before them, and Thorncress smoothed his hand down its velvet neck in a familiar gesture.

"You ought ride in front," he told Loxley. "You're looking yet unsteady on your feet."

He wasn't wrong. Loxley was half convinced he was still dreaming, his vision filled with shadowy, half-formed shapes and grasping fingers. But he was awake, and had been for some time. He shook his head, which did nothing to clear it. The sharp fear he felt within the ring had dissipated, and with it the adrenaline, leaving behind only a prickling unease.

"It's a strange sensation," he murmured to either Thorncress or the horse, which he approached with one hand outstretched to land upon the stirrup. "Was I enchanted, do you think? I must have been. But am I still? And why me?"

"I couldn't answer the former without taking a closer look at you, and this is no place for such examinations. As for the latter— Well. What have you done to attract attention from the Fair Folk?"

Loxley's insides went cold as ice. "Nothing," he whispered. "Surely— No, nothing." The muscle on the right side of his neck throbbed, suddenly hot and aching, and he rubbed it over his collar. The skin felt bruised. A dream of keen, watchful eyes flared in his memory, and he trembled all over for an instant before steadying himself with one hand on the pommel of the saddle.

Thorncress watched his every movement before stepping forward. "Here."

He helped Loxley into the saddle before climbing up behind him and taking the reins. He was comfortably warm against Loxley's back, the only warmth that Loxley could feel, in fact. The morning wasn't so very cold on its own, though the night had surely been, but what truly chilled him to the bone was the prospect of having caught the eye of some fae creature. The Folk had slipped into folklore and superstition centuries ago. What could he have done to draw such a being to him?

But such questions would only drive him mad. The fae hardly operated on human rationale, after all.

"Are you settled?" Thorncress' voice was a low rumble in Loxley's ear.

"I hardly know. Onward, and I'll warn you if I think I'm about to fall."

"That will do," said Thorncress, and they were away.

The ride was not nearly so fast or jarring as Loxley had expected, either because Thorncress was reluctant to rush his horse over the uneven ground or because he doubted Loxley's ability to stay in the saddle. Whichever it was, Loxley appreciated it, for as the ride progressed he became increasingly disoriented. His thoughts grew untethered and wandered far afield. Remaining upright proved a greater challenge than it ought, and if Thorncress were not behind him to provide a barrier, Loxley would surely have fallen as soon as the horse took its first step. As it was, Thorncress held him in place like a rock, and Loxley's mind roamed far and wide.

He had been dreaming earlier that night; he was sure of it. Images of a pale, slender creature bathed in moonlight flitted through his head, lingering in the corners of his eyes. It had been speaking to him, telling him secrets deep and dark and endlessly fascinating, if only he could remember. They were there on the tip of his tongue . . .

The wild heathers of the moors gradually gave way to a dirt road, and Loxley had never been gladder to see one. Though Thorncress might be at home in the northern wilds, Loxley was not, and wanted nothing more than to return home to London and burrow into his bed and stay there for a considerable time, until the mysterious happenings of the previous night were but a distant and harmless memory.

"The moors are not so bad," Thorncress said. "I think you would dislike the woods more."

"It's very possible," Loxley agreed, stifling a yawn, "but since I have not yet had occasion to wake up disoriented in the woods at the Folks' mercy, I shall settle for disliking the moors for now."

He felt Thorncress laugh behind him. "As you like."

"I do not like," Loxley informed him. "I like very little of this situation at all, save for you and your horse."

"I'm honoured."

"If I go to sleep, would you be so kind as to keep me from falling out of the saddle? Only, I don't think I can fight it for much longer, and I should very much like to avoid waking in another circle."

"I'm already the only thing keeping you astride the horse," Thorncress pointed out, "so, by all means, sleep. I'll wake you on our arrival."

"You are very generous," Loxley mumbled, tipping forward over the horse's neck as his body gave up the reins of consciousness and dropped him into an exhausted sleep. The last thing he knew was Thorncress wrapping one arm around his middle to keep him upright. Loxley leaned back against him, boneless and warm, and lost himself to hazy visions of slate grey skies and shapes that shimmered and lurked behind the clouds.

※ ※ ※

"Wake up, Mr. Loxley. You're back."

Loxley groaned and stirred. His return to consciousness was not a kind one. His eyes ached to open, his head throbbed, and his entire body hurt all over. He felt caught in the throes of both a terrible flu and a raucous hangover, though he was sure he'd been neither sick nor drinking the day before. He relayed all of this to Thorncress with one arm flung over his face to keep his eyes fixed firmly in their sockets, as they seemed keen on escaping.

"I'm sorry for it, sir, but you ought drink this before you sleep again."

Loxley pulled his arm away just enough to crack a suspicious glance at the drink in question.

"Just water, though I reckon you'll be hungry enough when you next wake."

Loxley accepted the glass, feeling rather like an invalid, though too sore and tired to find it humiliating. "I don't suppose you've uncovered who's responsible for my being in such a state," he said plaintively as Thorncress retrieved the glass and set it on the bedside table by the pitcher.

"No, but I'll find out soon enough." He stood back to regard Loxley with a critical eye. "Can you get undressed on your own? You'll feel worse if you sleep like that much longer."

Loxley flushed but took stock of himself. Thorncress had deposited him atop the covers in a small bed—in an inn, he assumed, though where it was or for how long they'd travelled, he couldn't guess. His clothes were in disarray from the ride and subsequent manhandling; Thorncress must have had to carry him to his room like a common drunk. Loxley would indeed regret sleeping in his coat and boots, and though his fingers were oddly uncooperative, he couldn't bear the thought of asking for further assistance.

"I'll be fine." Propping himself up against the headboard, he hoped he looked steadier than he felt. "What are a few buttons and laces after having escaped a faerie ring?"

"After having been rescued from one," Thorncress corrected, but otherwise seemed inclined to take Loxley at his word. Donning his hat, he nodded and turned for the door. "Sleep well, Mr. Loxley. I shall see you come morning. There are things we should discuss, when your head's in a better place for it."

Before Loxley could press him for details, he was gone, the door clicking shut behind him.

Loxley stared at the empty space where Thorncress had been before forcing himself from the bed. A basin of water stood on a small table opposite the foot of the bed, placid beneath a varnished mirror. He splashed a handful over his face, scrubbing away the lingering dirt. What he needed was a shave and a bath and a good night's sleep in his own bed; what he had was a washcloth, a basin of lukewarm water, and an unsettling sensation in the pit of his stomach that his waking in a faerie ring had not been a random accident at all. His neck gave a throb of pain at the thought. Frowning, he tugged his collar open to examine the skin in the mirror, turning his head in order to catch the dim lamplight.

A small bruise glared back at him, stark and luridly purple against the pale line of his throat. Perversely, his first instinct was to press his thumb against it, and he bit his lip at the immediate ache. It was obviously a fresh bruise: the purple was dark, almost black, and there was no fading to green or yellow around the edges. It was small and circular, sharply defined, as if something had taken his skin between its teeth and bitten down hard to break the capillaries. It must have hurt to receive such a mark, yet his memory remained troublingly blank.

Biting his lip, he swept the washcloth over it and resolved to wear his coat tightly buttoned until it faded. The thought of having others' eyes on it made him shrink, as if it were so private a part of him that he could share it with no one. Whatever the mark was, it belonged to him and him alone, and he was too tired to interrogate the source of that instinct, though it made him uneasy.

Shedding his coat and boots, he had just climbed back into bed when he paused. Sitting by the door, tucked away in the shadows, was his travel bag. He recognized it by the particular scuff mark on the leather; he'd carried it with him wherever he went for the past ten years. But Thorncress had said he would take him to the inn where *he* had been staying—so then why was Loxley's bag already there?

Creeping from the bed, Loxley dropped to his knees and opened the clasp, holding his breath against the fear of what he might find.

But there was nothing out of the ordinary. There were a few changes of clothes, his pack of toiletries, his journal and wallet, all nestled in quite innocently, as if he had packed for a few days' travel and then simply—lost his mind.

A sense of urgency nipped at him as he flipped through his journal, searching for the most recent entry. He used it to keep dates, for the most part, though sometimes he scrawled down marginal notes about books he meant to look up, or ideas for research he meant to pursue. But the last entry was a note for a lunch date with a colleague that he had attended on the tenth of November: it had been pleasant, but uneventful, and almost a week had passed after that before the hole in his memory gaped wide, swallowing his days.

He wasn't sure of the current date. How much time had he lost? Pressing the heels of his palms to his eyes, he willed the starbursts that erupted under the pressure to resolve into images and memories. He pressed until his eyes ached and anxiety gnawed at his insides, but there was no clarity to be found. Letting his hands drop, he looked helplessly to his journal.

"What happened to me?" he whispered.

But there was no explanation. Finally, after his knees began to protest from kneeling on the cold floor, he returned to bed, shuffling under the covers and turning off the bedside lamp, though it was still daylight. His head no sooner touched the pillow before he was lost, sinking back into sweet oblivion. He dreamed of dark strangers who carried exotic spices in their coat pockets, and of pale-eyed, cruel-lipped creatures with grasping fingers, watching him from the corners of the room.

※ ※ ※

Loxley slept through the last remains of the day and all through the night, occasionally waking from disorienting dreams, but never for long. It wasn't until the dawn sun was slanting through the curtains that he woke properly, brushing the cobwebs of sleep from his mind and the grit from his eyes. He felt as though he'd slept for years; his body was heavy and his mind was slow from it. It was tempting to sink back into the pillows and draw the covers high, ignoring the waking world in its entirety, but there were too many questions he needed answered, and he wouldn't find them in his dreams.

He dragged himself out of bed and into the sharp morning air, shivering as he dressed in fresh clothes from his bag, and donning his coat, which, after a second's hesitation, he buttoned to his throat. The bruise hadn't faded overnight; if anything, it looked darker, almost angry, and was infinitely tender to the touch.

"Damn it all anyway," he said to his reflection in the silvery mirror. "Damn bruises, damn faerie rings, and damn the moors."

It didn't make him feel better or bolder. With a sigh, he ran his hand through his curls, and set off downstairs to find something to eat and learn where, exactly, Thorncress had taken him.

"Mr. Loxley!" A plump, cherub-faced woman waved him over to the counter as soon as he rounded the bottom of the stairs. She had a matronly way to her, and vowels as flat and northern as Thorncress'. "Are you well, Mr. Loxley? Mr. Thorncress said you were taken ill, and you looked in such a state—are you much recovered, sir?"

"I—yes, I was taken with a fever," Loxley lied, "but I do feel better this morning, thank you, ma'am. But you must forgive me—the sickness has played tricks on my mind. Would you be so good as to tell me where I am, and when I got here?"

"Why, sir! You must be more scattered than you look. Sit down, sit." She ushered him into a chair across from her, refusing to go on until she was satisfied that he was settled. "This is the Red Fox Inn, Mr. Loxley, and I'm Mrs. Somerset. We spoke when you first arrived the evening before last, just afore you took ill."

"I didn't mention the nature of my travel?" he asked hopefully, but she shook her head.

"Not a word of it, sir. Only that you'd come from London. It's a ways to travel, especially by yourself. City-folk tend to find it lonely up in the north, so they say. All that wide-open space: it's like you forget what to do with yourself, away from the bustle of the city."

"I suppose that's true. I spent my childhood here, though I scarcely remember it."

"Ah, no, sir. If it's in your bones, it'll come back to you. If the north was ever in your blood, it'll stay there." She looked him over. "Breakfast, then? It'll put some colour back in your cheeks."

"Please." Loxley glanced around, but the inn was deserted besides the two of them. "Is Mr. Thorncress still here? He said we were to talk this morning, but perhaps I've missed him."

"He's not come down yet, sir. He was ever so kind taking care of you the other day, though you wouldn't think it to look at him."

"He was most generous, helping me as he did."

"He stops by once a year or so. Has done for ages, now. He spends most of his days out wandering the wilds, you know, with nary a soul for company but that horse. I suppose they're used to it, those Gypsy types. I could never go so long without a place to call home. Do you know him?"

"I never met him before yesterday, but I find myself much indebted to him now," Loxley said pointedly.

Mrs. Somerset nodded, seemingly oblivious to his distaste for her gossip. "He's a good man, despite it all. Ah: speak of the devil! Good morning, Mr. Thorncress. I've got a pot of porridge on, if you'd like. Or tea?"

If Thorncress had heard her comments, he gave no sign of it. Perhaps he was used to such whispers dogging his heels. "Both, please."

Thorncress looked as Loxley remembered him: tall and dark, his presence greater than the sum of his parts, shrouded all in black and looking as if he had just wandered in from the wilds rather than come downstairs from a night spent in a soft bed. And now that Loxley was in less of a haze, he noticed other things, besides: like the quiet intelligence in Thorncress' dark eyes, and the circles under them that spoke of perpetual fatigue.

"You survived the night, then," Thorncress observed.

"I did, though I was troubled by strange dreams."

"Hm." Thorncress gestured for Loxley to follow him to a table in the corner, where the glow of morning light couldn't reach them. Sitting, he leaned in, his elbows braced on the tabletop as he studied Loxley's face. "Tell me about them."

"They were barely more than images. I had the feeling of being watched again, like I told you before, and trees—there aren't trees like that in London. I must have been dreaming of my childhood home."

"Did you come north to visit it?"

"No, no. My parents lived in London until they passed. There's no one for me here."

"I'm sorry for it. You never saw one of the Fair Folk as a child?"

"No, never! I would remember that." Loxley paused. "Wouldn't I?"

Thorncress shrugged, never taking his gaze from Loxley's face. "I couldn't say. But Faerie's left a mark on you all the same. I can smell it. Old magic, like frost and blood. It's clinging to you, even now."

Loxley froze, his tongue cleaving to his palate. Thorncress couldn't have seen the mark on his neck; he would question Loxley outright if he had.

Mrs. Somerset chose that moment to bustle over with their breakfast, two steaming bowls of thick oats doused in milk and honey. It smelled hearty, and though Loxley hadn't eaten in longer than he could remember, his stomach turned over from anxiety, pushing the hunger aside.

"What should I do?" His voice cracked on the question.

"Go home to London. Stay away from the north. Get further, if you can." One corner of Thorncress' mouth twitched, though there was nothing funny about it. "Try the Americas, perhaps."

"America!"

"You'll not find a scrap of faerie magic there."

"I won't find much of anything there," Loxley countered. "England is my home. I'll find some other way to free myself from this enchantment."

"It should wear off in its own time, if you can escape Faerie's attention for that long."

That, at least, was reassuring.

"It can find me in London, though. What else but fae influence could have persuaded me to come north?"

Thorncress set into his breakfast. "Get yourself some protection. Cold iron or charms, something to keep them at bay until they lose interest."

"Will they lose interest?" Loxley demanded.

Another shrug. "The Folk are flighty creatures. They could forget you tomorrow or follow you to your grave. There's no way of knowing."

"That's not helpful," Loxley snapped, and then immediately shut his mouth. "I apologize, sir. This isn't your fault."

"No, it's not."

"I owe you my life already; you must forgive me. It's been . . ." He shook his head. "I feel untethered. You're right. I should return to London and take what precautions I can there. I'll arrange a carriage and leave as soon as I'm able."

"You should eat, first."

"I know."

He poked at his porridge, willing his stomach to settle, and though he eventually managed to swallow it down, it tasted like ash in his mouth. As he came to the bottom of his bowl, Thorncress readied to leave.

"Thank you again," Loxley said, "for everything. If there's anything I can do—"

"Don't mention it," Thorncress said gruffly. "Don't go wandering into any more faerie rings, and I'll consider your debt repaid." Standing and adjusting his coat, he paused, looking down at him. "Take care, Mr. Loxley. And don't come north again."

※ ※ ※

Sitting in the back of the carriage as it rumbled its way to London, Loxley stared blankly out the window, his hands in his pockets to ward off the chill. Whatever state he'd been in leaving the city, he hadn't thought to pack his gloves or a scarf, and the November air was far too cool to abide without. What on earth had possessed him?

As the landscape rolled by, grey on grey, Loxley could admit to a certain beauty in such stark scenery. It looked more forbidding than he remembered it as a child, but perhaps his memories were touched by nostalgia, adding warmth and colour where there had never been. But then, he hadn't been raised on the moors themselves. His childhood home had bordered a wood to the south of Yorkshire, and great trees had grown in the backyard, amid the wildflowers and the stinging nettles. He had spent hours there every day, at least until the frost set in deep and the cold drove him indoors.

Looking back, he was unsure what age he had been when his parents had moved him south. Young enough to have had few friends or attachments. For an instant, it seemed that his absent memories predated his misadventure on the moors, and wide swaths of his boyhood were likewise missing from his mind. But it was natural, surely, for adults to remember little of their childhoods. There was nothing unusual in the sparse images that made up his youngest years.

In his pocket, his thumb brushed over something hard and smooth, and he frowned, pulling it out. A hawthorn apple sat in the middle of his palm, petrified into a smooth, hard sphere. Its skin had darkened to a deep, rich red, almost black, with a single indentation at the top that marked where its stem had once fastened it to its branch.

He had used to collect haws, as a boy. The trees—

The carriage jolted to a stop as the horses shrieked, and Loxley lurched in his seat, catching his balance against the door. Opening it, he poked his head around, calling to the driver, "What's happened?"

"Sorry, sir: the horses spooked at something in the road. I'll have them righted in a moment."

He could hear the animals huffing and stomping their hooves, but whatever had upset them, the driver didn't seem concerned. Perhaps a rabbit had dashed underfoot, or a deer. Loxley sat back, his brow furrowed as he ran his thumb over the haw's hard skin, turning it over and over in his hand like a worry stone. A short burst of wind whined at the window, and he shivered, though he couldn't feel it.

Something scratched against the door, a thin and creaking sound.

Tree branches, he thought, distantly. Barren branches, like the ones that used to scratch at his bedroom window through the night.

Except that there were no trees by the roadside, nothing but the empty stretch of moorland.

William…

The mark on his neck ached with sudden intensity and he raised his hand to cover it, burning hot and shaking with chills. The thing outside the carriage scratched again, asking to be let in.

CHAPTER TWO

THESE RESTLESS DREAMS

Loxley slipped in and out of consciousness like a fish skimming just below the surface of the water, being rushed downstream against his will. The waking world was bright and painful and he shied away from it, preferring the deep, dark calm of slumber. There were things above the surface that he wanted to avoid: things with sharp teeth and cold fingers and terrible, biting kisses that tasted like frost against his lips, making his skin crawl and his stomach churn with terror.

Down at the bottom of the river he endeavoured to bury himself in the black mud, where he might rest undisturbed for the next century, until the danger passed.

It's a trick, whispered some unbroken part of his mind. *It's a lie.*

He turned uneasily.

Wake up before it's too late. His thoughts took on a flat, northern affect, rough and gravelly and somehow familiar. *Wake up before it gets worse.*

Loxley opened his eyes. For an indeterminate time, he couldn't say whether he was awake or dreaming: the world seemed trapped behind a veil, hazy and unknowable, and he couldn't see how to part it. When he tried to speak, his tongue was thick and heavy in his mouth, and his limbs leaden and uncooperative. Such a state should call for panic, but, like a rabbit trapped in the serpent's coils, it seemed the struggle was already over.

He slept again.

He couldn't classify what he saw as dreams, but rather as fevered images of a half-conscious mind on the verge of waking. There was a great black stallion with a billowing mane like the ocean's waves and hooves like flint, which struck sparks where they touched the ground, and his rider was cloaked all in black, carrying the sun like a weapon. A long-legged creature made of frost and starlight crouched before the horse, its eyes reflecting the empty moon and its back covered in a thousand wings, all glitteringly iridescent like a beetle's, clicking and whirring in terrible cacophony.

The horse and rider charged, and the creature reared up, a million tiny, needle-sharp teeth bared. Loxley knew what those teeth felt like, buried in his skin.

He himself was mired deep in the earth, black soil covering his legs as ancient roots rose from beneath to hold him in place. Frost bit at his fingertips and froze his lungs when he tried to speak.

A second or a moment or a century passed. When he next opened his eyes, the rider was kneeling beside him, one hand on his face. The touch was too hot—the rider seemed adorned in a crown of flames, flickering white in the pale moonlight—or was that the sun rising behind him? —and Loxley shrank back, too used to the cold. Frowning, the rider spoke, but his words were incomprehensible to Loxley's fevered mind.

"I can't hear you," he tried to say. "I'm too deep in the earth."

This only seemed to trouble the rider further, and because Loxley could neither understand nor help him, he lost his tie to the waking world, and slipped under once more.

The next time he woke, he was on horseback, slumped over the beast's neck as Thorncress held him in place from behind.

"Here we are again," Loxley murmured, too weak to move, his cheek pressed to the horse's rough mane. "What time is this? How many times have we . . ."

"Are you awake?"

"I don't think so. If I am, I would prefer not to be. How do you keep finding me?" He didn't expect a reply.

Thorncress seemed to dislike speculation or straight answers, and Loxley was too tired to press him for one.

"I can feel the magic on you." Thorncress sounded vexed, as if Loxley had pressed him after all. "It calls to me, all the way across the moors, as if it were a shining beacon I'm helpless to resist."

"I'm dreaming," Loxley said certainly. "You would never admit to helplessness in anything. You are like a stone, sir: impenetrable."

Thorncress huffed a laugh, sounding rueful. "Oh, I may surprise you."

"I'll take back the narrative of my own dreams now, thank you." Before Thorncress could reply, Loxley fell unconscious once more.

※ ※ ※

It was dark, and in the sliver of a second it took for his mind to locate his body and account for all his limbs, Loxley lay very still, afraid that when he opened his eyes he would be outside again, with the frost creeping in close all around.

He forced himself out from under the thick trappings of sleep to find himself back in his room at the Red Fox, as if he had never left it. To his left stood the bedside table with the lamp, and before him, the stretch of bed piled high with quilts and blankets to ward off the chill. To his right, the window, with its shabby curtains drawn, beneath which stood a solitary chair on which his coat lay neatly folded, and between that chair and the far wall, tucked into the darkest corner of the room, sat Thorncress.

He was little more than a silhouette. Though it was too dark to pick out details, Loxley traced his form with his gaze: from the top of his head, where his hair fell in loose, tangled waves over his shoulders, to his chest, where the heavy lines of his coat disappeared into the chair. Shapes only made sense again further down: a knee, and then a boot, resting solidly against the floor. Thorncress didn't look like he had moved in hours, planted there at an angle to keep Loxley in his sights: Loxley, the door, and the window.

"You're awake." Thorncress' voice was rough, as if he hadn't slept in some time.

"So it seems." Loxley pushed himself to his elbows, wincing as his head throbbed with the movement. The blankets pooled around his lap, and he found that he had been put to bed in his underclothes. The thought of Thorncress undressing him left him feeling shy and indecent now that the enchantment was fading from his mind. Thorncress would have made short work of his buttons, deft fingers easily freeing them and shedding his layers, his hands firm and straightforward against his skin—

Loxley banished the thought before the old familiar fear could take hold.

"What happened? I don't remember another faerie ring, but then, my memory doesn't seem to belong to me of late."

"You were very nearly lost, this time. When I got there, something had its hooks deep in you. I drove it off, but couldn't kill it. Do you recall any of your encounter?"

A press of tongue, the bite of teeth, and the bone-deep ache of clinging frost.

"I can't be sure. So much of it still seems a fever dream. I was on the road back to London, and there were trees— No, we were on the moors, still. But I heard branches scraping against the carriage door, the way they used to scratch at my bedroom window when I was a boy, and . . ." His gaze drifted to his coat. Was that haw still in his pocket? "Will it happen again, do you think?"

"I expect so, seeing as the creature has not yet got what it wants from you, and you've yet to give it sufficient cause to leave you be."

A hot flush swept through Loxley. "Are you suggesting it's my own fault that this creature has sought me out?"

"No. That's not what I meant."

"Because I assure you, I should most certainly like to give it cause to avoid me, if only so you can save yourself the trouble of coming to my rescue yet again. But as I know of no way to deter the Fair Folk from their course, you must either excuse or instruct me."

"I didn't mean to suggest that you are to blame," Thorncress said wearily. "The Folk will act as they see fit, with no regard for us mere mortals."

"Then what am I meant to do?" Loxley asked desperately. "You seem to know the art of drawing them off and breaking their spells—will you not teach me?"

"It's an art hard won, and not easily taught." Thorncress raised one hand to stem the tide of Loxley's protests. "But I'll not abandon you, so long as you remain in danger."

Loxley put on a brave face. "You must think me a proper damsel in distress," he said, aiming for levity and falling short. "How many times have you had to rescue me now? I seem utterly incapable of looking after myself. I fear I must cut a pathetic figure next to the likes of you."

"I don't think of you as a damsel whatsoever, and there's no shame in being bested by the fae. Stronger men than you have been stolen away, yet you remain."

"Only thanks to you."

Thorncress shrugged. "I won't argue. But you judge yourself too harshly."

But Thorncress wouldn't have frozen like that under the enchantment. Loxley's life had long been defined by such paralysis, but its familiarity made it no easier to bear.

Before Loxley could reply, a wavering cry cut through the night, eerie and thin-sounding through the walls. For a bare second, Thorncress hesitated—the only time Loxley had ever seen him less than certain of his actions—before crossing to the window, drawing the curtain aside to peer out into the darkness.

"Is it dogs?" Loxley asked. The cry didn't sound quite right, but then, he was used to London's noises, not the animal sounds of the countryside.

Thorncress didn't move for another minute, until the cries had faded off into the distance. "Just dogs," he finally said, in a tone Loxley couldn't parse. Turning back to Loxley, he said, "The creature. Did it do you any harm, before I arrived?"

Loxley could still feel the cold press of the creature's tongue against his lips, the scrape of its nails and the cold touch of its body where it held him close. "I'm unharmed, but I'd prefer to avoid meeting it again." He shivered, his stomach tightening with fear and shame, and he dropped his gaze to his fingers, twining them together on top of the sheets. "Can't you fix me? With all your knowledge of magic, can you not just . . ."

"The enchantment will fade once the cause is rooted out. A more direct application of magic could do you more harm than good."

Loxley frowned, untangling himself from the sheets and sitting on the edge of the bed as he tugged his clothes on. "You said I ought to carry iron on me, or some manner of charm. Should I carry a knife, or some such weapon? Only, I don't know if I could actually kill the thing, even if I could keep my wits about me. I've never killed anything more than a fly, before." The thought of killing a living being, or even attempting to, seemed overwhelming. He had always been given to gentleness and harboured an aversion to conflict, and the prospect of such violence made him shiver with apprehension, his insides cold and squirming.

"I'd not advise you carry a knife. I fear you'd prove a greater danger to yourself than your opponent."

Loxley didn't bother to feign offense; Thorncress was entirely correct. "But I must do something. I can't sit here idly waiting for it to spirit me away again. What if next time you can't hear my call, or can't reach me in time? I've no wish to be trapped in Faerie, and I've no wish to be this creature's plaything. It's never given me the slightest choice in the matter, and I don't want—" Useless tears stung his eyes and he brushed them aside before Thorncress could see him cry.

"The Fair Folk never ask permission for much, but I don't think your creature is one of them. Not properly, anyway."

"How do you mean?"

"Finish getting dressed, Mr. Loxley, and meet me downstairs. Then we shall see what you know of changelings."

CHAPTER THREE

THE LOXLEY HOUSE

"Changelings," said Loxley. "Are they not children?"

They sat opposite one another at a secluded table downstairs, their breakfasts spread between them. Dawn had broken pale and grey, her fingers slipping over the horizon with such subtlety that it seemed like the sun might not rise at all, and leave the world caught in the dim wash of watercolour half-light.

"They start as children," Thorncress said. "Most of them die that way, too. The Fair Folk take a healthy human child and leave behind one of their own in its place—something sickly and doomed to die, oft before the parents realize there's anything amiss."

Loxley had never heard any consensus on what happened to children once they were stolen away to Faerie. A common theory was that they were used to pay a tithe to Hell, for land rented from that place. Maybe they were raised as fae and never knew anything different, though that seemed optimistic. He didn't ask if Thorncress knew the truth; if he did, Loxley wasn't sure he wanted to hear it.

"You think my creature was a changeling child. How can you tell?"

"I interrupted it last night; the magic was thick in the air, the circle growing all around you. Do you know what happens to a body if left in a faerie ring?"

"Nothing good." Of that much, Loxley was certain.

Thorncress snorted. "Indeed not. The Folk open a door between their world and ours, and steal the person away. It's a trap for us and an offering to them."

Loxley studied that from every angle. "Why not take me to Faerie itself?"

Thorncress took a swig of tea, black and unsweetened. "I don't think it can. Either it doesn't remember or it never learned how to cross between the worlds. It's left stumbling in the dark, trying to find its way blind." Thorncress eyed him. "You needn't pity it. It's still fae, whatever its circumstance. It'll suck you dry and leave you an empty husk without thinking twice."

"I don't pity it. But I do pity the loneliness that situation must breed. I should be made of stone if I did not."

"You might endeavour to be more like stone, at least until this creature has been dealt with."

Loxley poked at his porridge. "More like you, you mean."

Thorncress looked at him oddly. "Is that what you think of me?" He shook his head before Loxley could respond. "Fine. Be more like me. The creature will kill you or worse if you don't end it first, so steel yourself to that purpose. By whatever means necessary."

"I didn't mean to insult you—"

"It's no matter. You're not wrong."

"I was always given to sympathy," Loxley said softly. "Stone and steel do not come easily to me, but I shall try."

"You must."

They both fell silent for a moment, picking at their food. Loxley was the first to speak.

"What I don't understand is why it chose me. There must be something that I did, or something it saw in me, to have attracted it. But I've lived in London since I was a boy. I never had any intention of returning north. I barely thought of it."

"Did you have any siblings, growing up?"

Loxley looked at him sharply. "You think— But no. I was an only child."

The second, more tantalizing option, hung between them unspoken. If Loxley himself had been stolen as a babe—if he, here and now, were not William Loxley at all, but an unwitting imposter—would that not explain a lifetime of peculiarities? Would it not excuse certain inclinations, if he could say that he was not human, and thus not bound to human law or nature?

He could not bring himself to ask such a thing aloud.

Thorncress eyed him with some speculation, but did not put the possibility to words. "I think you ought return to your childhood home, either way, and see if there's anything that may have escaped your notice at the time."

"I don't even know if it's still standing."

"Find out."

"You no longer suggest I return immediately to London?"

"I no longer believe it's possible. That creature has marked you."

Loxley's hand twitched with the sudden urge to cover his neck, though the bruise was hidden under his collar. Thorncress tracked the movement with keen eyes, but he didn't comment on it.

"Very well." Loxley swallowed his fear. "I'll arm myself with cold iron and . . ."

"I could accompany you," Thorncress offered slowly, "if you allow it."

"You—what?"

"I may be the only soul capable of fending this thing off. And I will confess to an interest in seeing this unfold. So, if you are amenable, I would go with you."

"As my protector," Loxley said dumbly.

Thorncress shrugged. "If you like."

"It must be a powerful interest, to inconvenience yourself to such an extent."

"It's not inconvenient. Obviously, I make a study of faerie magic. Your case is of interest to me." He took a long drink. "*You* are of interest to me."

Loxley flushed to his roots and hid behind his own drink for a moment. When he had recovered, he set it down on the table and gave a definitive nod. "Very well. I accept your proposal, Mr. Thorncress. We shall go to my old house, if it's still standing, and see . . . whatever we shall see."

※ ※ ※

Thorncress wasted no time in putting their plan in motion; they left the Red Fox Inn directly after breakfast. He bought Loxley a horse, ignoring his stammered protests, as well as the hat, scarf, and gloves that he had neglected to take from London, and they rode south for Pickering at once. Loxley, who had not ridden a horse in many years, and certainly not for any extended length of time, was at first occupied with staying in the saddle, and then with grimly anticipating the sore muscles that would greet him the next day. But eventually those preoccupations wore away, and he nudged his horse to walk at Thorncress' side.

"How did you come to know so much about faerie magic? You called it an art hard won, but even here, the Folk are not commonly acknowledged."

"They're best not acknowledged at all, lest you wish to draw them down on you."

"Then how did you fall into this line of study?"

Thorncress was silent for so long that Loxley thought he wouldn't answer at all, until—

"You said your parents had passed already, and that you have no siblings. Are you married, Mr. Loxley?"

Loxley twisted sharply to face him, but Thorncress' expression was impassive, staring at the road ahead.

"I'm not, sir. I've no family to speak of, neither by blood nor marriage."

Thorncress was silent for a moment longer. "Necessity," he said at length, "will drive a man to learn any manner of things. Necessity, and love."

He didn't speak again, and Loxley didn't know how to break the silence that followed. Instead, he let his horse fall back to follow Thorncress, and studied how the man and the landscape complemented one another. Both beautiful in their severity, and given to grey moods. Was it grief, then, that coloured Thorncress so? Loxley didn't wish to pry or ask for more than he was offered, though the curiosity burned at him.

He wanted to ask if Thorncress was married, but oh, how Loxley despised that question. He'd been asked it often enough, over the years: he was of prime marrying age, after all, and after a certain point, one's bachelorhood became suspicious. People asked him knowingly, at times, and those were the worst: when he could see the speculation as to his nature dancing in their eyes, just out of reach of their tongue. There had been no such speculation in Thorncress' tone, but then, he seemed overwhelmingly averse to gossip. Loxley was grateful for it. There was no reason for the man to suspect, so long as Loxley was careful.

But he was so very tired of being careful. It was only his fear of the noose that kept him so— But perhaps that was a lie. He feared Thorncress' judgement, as well.

Sighing, he turned his gaze from Thorncress to the sky. It threatened rain, the clouds rolling so low he could almost touch them, slow and ponderous like giants turning in their beds. The clouds were impenetrable, as they were in all of England, but on clearer days, Loxley sometimes thought that he could see something in the sky, or rather, behind it, like a trick with lights and mirrors. But this sky was dark and thunderous, and soon the rain would break and he'd be able to see nothing at all.

※ ※ ※

Pickering was a small town of perhaps three thousand, bordered by Dalby Forest to the north, on the edge of which stood Loxley's childhood home. As they rode through the little market square, Pickering Castle loomed ahead of them, its towers stunted and neglected, though largely unaffected by the centuries. The sight of it stirred Loxley's memories: the old stone walls had been a permanent feature of his childhood, constantly looming on the edge of town, and returning to its shadow felt like returning to the company of an old, half-forgotten friend.

Like the castle, the Loxley house stood empty. Where it had once been comforting it was now weather-worn and fallen to disrepair, its windows dark and its siding stripped of colour. Birds nested in the eaves, and animals denned beneath the porch. The sight filled Loxley with a strange melancholy, though he hadn't thought of the place in years.

"My parents sold the house when we moved," he said, dismounting from his horse to approach the front gate in cautious wonder. "I had thought it would still have tenants."

Thorncress didn't shift from his saddle. "Looks like it's been abandoned a while, now."

"It was a perfectly good house. What could have caused anyone to leave it without selling?"

As Loxley lifted the latch, the gate groaned, old iron gone to rust and reluctant to move from its bed. It opened only under considerable force, and when Loxley stepped through, the weeds and nettles of the overgrown yard immediately wrapped themselves around his ankles, biting into his trousers as if urging him to stay in place. Grimacing, he shook free, following what had once been a cobblestone path to the front door.

"Are you coming?" he asked over his shoulder, one hand on the door.

"I've a mind to see the back," Thorncress replied, still astride his horse.

"The yard?" A memory threatened to uncurl. Loxley frowned. "But that's just trees."

"You're always talking about them. Branches at your windowpane. You've mentioned dreaming it enough times."

Loxley hesitated at the front door, his fingers curled around the handle. "That's true . . ."

Thorncress studied him. "You don't wish to go there."

That was true also, but for the life of him, Loxley couldn't articulate why.

Frowning, Thorncress held out one arm. "Come."

Burning with trepidation, Loxley returned to his side. Thorncress finally dismounted, and, leaving the horses to nose through the weeds, he took Loxley's arm and led him firmly around the house to the back. There, the woods pressed in close, reclaiming the yard for themselves, dotting the once-orderly lawn with saplings and tangled weeds that grew as tall as a man. The trees' skeleton branches still clung to their papered leaves. Tall, dark trunks that stood like shadows, and beneath, a thick carpet of rot and fallen hawthorn apples.

"Tell me what you remember," Thorncress said. "Why don't you want to be back here?"

"I used to play here." The haw burned like a weight in his pocket. "It was always rather given to weeds, and the nettles grew up around the tree trunks in the autumn, but nothing to this extent."

"This is years of neglect." Thorncress nodded to the saplings that stood whip-like in the yard. "A decade, at least."

In another decade, Dalby Forest would overtake the house entirely, but the line where the yard had once ended was still visible, marked by great, old trees that towered above the younger ones. A single hawthorn stood among them, its branches spread wide, like a king among commoners. Loxley shivered.

"We could find some public record in the town hall," Thorncress said, watching Loxley closely, "to learn why the last owners left."

"We could," Loxley agreed, staring past Thorncress into the line of trees. Something flickered, like a shadow, and he flinched.

Thorncress turned to look.

"It was nothing," Loxley said, one hand pressed over his heart. "I thought I saw— But it was nothing. A rabbit, or a fox."

Thorncress frowned into the woods, one hand still wrapped around Loxley's wrist. "Tell me where you used to play. Did you ever go into the woods?"

"Hardly at all. Just where the trees came into the yard. I never wandered far . . ."

Loxley took a halting step forward, his fingers restless like he wanted to reach for something, though he didn't know what. The haws on the ground, nestled amid the fallen leaves, shone like rubies dropped from a careless hand. His gaze wandered to the trees, searching for something among their trunks, hidden under the stinging nettles—

He shook his head. The memories hurt, like straining to see something in the dark, and he felt strangely exposed, trying to uncover them in Thorncress' presence. The other man didn't belong there, in that overgrown yard. The hawthorn wasn't for him to see.

"Let's go inside," Loxley said, tugging on Thorncress' grip. "I'm sure I can remember where all the rooms used to be—perhaps my old bedroom will give us something more useful."

Thorncress grunted but allowed himself to be guided to the back door and into the lonely little house.

It was dark inside, the floorboards rotting from seasons of damp, and a thick layer of dust coated every surface. Like walking into a mausoleum, Loxley held his breath, reluctant to disturb the slightest thing. There was little left of the house to match his scant memories. No fire burned in the hearth; no dinner cooked on the stove. The rocking chair where his mother used to sit and read was gone, and no jars of hawthorn apple jelly lined the pantry shelves. His bedroom was likewise abandoned, with nothing of his boyhood left behind. It left Loxley with a hollow sadness, an ache for how things used to be. He'd been happy, then. But London had carved away the quiet north and replaced it with the soot and clamour of city life, and he hadn't the time or space to harbour nostalgia.

Not until now.

"Am I supposed to feel something? If there is something here, tying me to Faerie, should I know it?"

"You might recognize it. It could rouse some deep-buried memory in you."

"It just feels lonely. The whole house. It's not made to stand empty. It doesn't have any purpose if it's not lived in, does it?"

"I'll warrant enough animals have made this place their home, over the years. You don't feel anything else?"

Loxley rolled the words around on his tongue, but every time he tried to speak of the hawthorn tree in the yard or the apple in his pocket, they suddenly slipped down his throat and out of reach. Frustration rolled off him in waves, but there was nothing he could do to articulate it.

"Nothing," he bit out. "Just this terrible loneliness."

"We'll spend the night," Thorncress finally said. "If there is something here, you'll draw it out."

"Is that wise?"

Thorncress fixed him with a flat stare. "Since you can't remember any more, it's necessary, even if it's not wise. Don't worry. I don't plan to let you out of my sight."

Loxley's skin prickled. Before, he would have taken comfort in that, and not only for the shameful thrill that came from having the attention of such a man. But in his old house, with the unsettling feeling of being watched raising the hairs on the back of his neck, his skin too tight and itching with unease, it sounded like a threat.

"Fine," he said shortly. "But we leave at first light."

Thorncress inclined his head. "As you like."

The beds were musty, the sheets untouched for years, moth-eaten and layered in dust. Loxley shook the blankets out in the yard, coughing as swirls of dust rose from them. The wind whispered to him from the tree branches, beckoning him further into the yard. The shadows from the woods stretched long and black in the evening light as the sky streaked grey with heavy clouds overhead.

He darted back inside, dragging the blankets with him, before the whispering wind could solidify and call his name.

Thorncress had cleared the worst of the debris from the hearth and lit a small fire, which crackled pitifully amid the damp wood, but it would do for the night. He had also dragged a solitary bed from one of the rooms to stand before the fireplace, rather than fight the old house with its many drafts.

Loxley fit the bedsheets over the mattress, his shoulders drawn tight, still expecting to hear his name come rattling through the windows.

"Are we sharing the bed tonight?" he asked, forcing his voice to a lighter tone, "or are you sleeping in a chair again?"

"The chair will do me fine."

Loxley swallowed his disappointment and tried to find the balance between genuine concern and giving himself away. It would never do to seem too eager to get a man into his bed, even if only for sleeping. "You'll be cold. This fire is enough to take the bite from the air, but it won't grow strong enough to warm you through."

"The cold doesn't bother me so easily as that."

Loxley bit his tongue against any further arguments. Thorncress was always brusque, but he seemed annoyed. He could tell Loxley was holding back about the trees, perhaps—but Loxley couldn't explain that he had no choice in the matter, that some other force was stopping his tongue. The hawthorn tree—

He couldn't voice any of it. Thorncress had every right to be annoyed. He was going so far out of his way, sacrificing time and comfort both for Loxley's sake, and Loxley couldn't even force himself to cooperate. He couldn't force his tongue to spit out the details of his curse, the haw or the bruise, any more than he could force himself not to look at Thorncress in that way.

"The nature of this enchantment," he began, not knowing what his next words would be, as if that could circumnavigate the infuriating speechlessness. "Do you think—"

But his throat closed tight and he was choked into silence. By the hearth, Thorncress waited, frowning.

"Sorry," Loxley said, coughing into his sleeve. "It must be all this dust."

"What were you going to ask?"

"I don't know."

Thorncress sighed and settled into a great armchair that had once been handsome, before the moths had got to it. "Go to sleep, Mr. Loxley. I'll see you safe to dawn. And try to remember what dreams you have, since we have little else to go on."

Swallowing a snappish retort, Loxley piled himself into bed, drawing the blankets to his chin. The fire was the only source of light, crackling in the hearth and casting the room in flickering shadows and an orange glow. Staring over the end of the bed and into the open flames, he imagined a shape there, like a creature hunched amid the logs and soot, watching him with pale, dancing eyes. Sleep crept up on him despite his desire to stay awake, and as his eyes fell shut, the wind whispered and whined through the walls.

William...

Loxley roused himself, blinking sleepily into the shadows. "Did you call my name?"

Thorncress looked at him sharply. "No."

He stifled his yawn. The heavy calm that weighed him down was much preferable to the panic he should have felt. "Ah. It must have been the wind. No matter—this house was always so drafty, it might as well be having conversations with itself."

"Mr. Loxley. Can you hear something? Is it speaking to you?"

"No, no. Only an overactive imagination and the house creaking, as it does. It's always been like this."

Thorncress' frown deepened. "That's what troubles me."

"I'm sure it's nothing." Loxley burrowed deeper into his blankets. "Good night, Mr. Thorncress. I trust you to safeguard me. You can drive back all manner of demons with your glare alone, I'm sure."

"Mr. Loxley—"

Thorncress' voice sounded like it was coming from over a great distance. Loxley frowned, but couldn't open his eyes. That should have been troubling—had he ever been so ill-rested before in his life? —but he couldn't muster the energy to be disturbed.

"I'm sorry, but we'll have to talk in the morning. I can't . . . I can't seem to stay awake."

Though he was dimly aware of Thorncress saying something in return, his tone urgent, it wasn't enough to keep him from slipping under the thick blanket of sleep. Clouds rolled over his mind and sank into the heart of him, like autumn frost sinking into the earth, and he was gone.

CHAPTER FOUR

ROUGH SLEEP

"You came back," the creature whispered, its voice thin and sharp as a knife, yet childlike in its wonder. "My prince, my boy, back home again."

It was a slender thing, pale as moonlight, with great opal eyes and long, spider-like fingers that ended in nails that skittered over Loxley's skin, sending shivers to wrack his frame. It was naked like an animal, and it moved like one: creeping up onto the bed on all fours, full of predatory grace, but its skin was smooth and hairless, and it was strangely androgynous, such that Loxley didn't know to call it male or female. He couldn't call it a man or woman, certainly, for it was so far from human that such titles made no sense.

"What are you?" he whispered, his voice soundless in the dark.

The creature smiled, its mouth full of needle-sharp teeth, bright as moonlight. "You remember, yes? We played together, you and I. Telling me stories, keeping me company. Such company—never again, never again. It left with you, left all alone, again and again. You remember?"

It lifted Loxley's right hand between its two, uncurling his index finger to press cold lips over the thin white scar. Loxley flinched back, as much from the cold as from the touch, but the creature only smiled wider and held him fast.

"I don't remember you," he said breathlessly. "What do you want from me?"

The creature frowned for the first time, its brows drawing in and its eyes flashing dangerously. "I waited for you. So long, I waited. You called me friend, then. Friends give each other favours."

Loxley's heart thudded sickly behind his ribs, dropping so suddenly he nearly retched. "I've promised no favours to Faerie." Tugging out of the creature's grasp, he twisted around to see past it, to the hearth—but Thorncress' chair stood abandoned, as if he had never been there at all.

"Am I dreaming?" Loxley asked desperately. "I must be! What have you done?"

"Come away," the creature urged, its fingers stroking through Loxley's hair, skittering over his cheeks and his neck like insect legs. "Come away, oh human child . . ."

"Why are you doing this?"

"Because you were kind to me, William Loxley. You told me your name and you called me friend."

With a smile like a razorblade, the creature snaked in and pressed its mouth to Loxley's throat, where the bruise was livid against his pale skin. For a second, there was nothing but the wet pressure of an open-mouthed kiss, only missing the warmth of human touch—and then the creature bit down, its teeth digging in like pinpricks, and Loxley tried to shout, but it came out only as a shocked gasp.

The world tilted on its axis and for one dizzying second, Loxley was blind, as if his skull was stuffed with cotton, his eye sockets empty. His stomach lurched as if he were falling from a great height—his heart dropped in time—

And he woke flailing out from under the bedsheets, his limbs tangled, as Thorncress tore the creature off him with a snarl, throwing it to the floor. Loxley struggled upright, one hand pressed over his wild heart, to stare as the creature crouched low, teeth bared in a hiss. Thorncress towered over it, his face thunderous.

"You cannot have him," he growled.

"He's bound to me," the creature snapped back, bristling.

For a second, Loxley saw the creature as if a glass slide were superimposed over the room. In the first image, the creature was the pale, androgynous thing it had first seemed, with scratching fingers and biting teeth. But in the new image, which flickered as if in uncertain reflection, it was tall and elegant, with a great many eyes that glowed like moonstones, and a host of glittering wings at its back.

The image shattered as Thorncress started forward, biting out strange words in a language Loxley didn't understand, but which smelled like incense and orange rind, and which made the creature hiss and spit as it slunk back.

"You can't have him," Thorncress repeated, his glare like daggers, and the creature flashed its teeth in a snarl or a smile as it darted past him, flickering like lightning, to press itself against the darkened window.

"He's mine already."

It lifted the latch and slipped through the opening before Thorncress could catch it, disappearing into the night-shrouded yard.

For an instant, neither of them moved, panting as they fought to regain their breaths—Loxley from terror, and Thorncress from the exertion of whatever magic he had employed to drive the creature off. Loxley was the first to break the stillness. He rose from the bed, pulling himself into his coat and boots and gathering his things, keeping his head down as he shouldered past Thorncress for the door. Thorncress followed a step behind him, still dressed from the evening, his mood stormy. Neither spoke as Thorncress retrieved the horses and saddled them; neither spoke until they were both mounted, the animals restless and recalcitrant from being interrupted before dawn.

"Mr. Loxley."

Loxley drew his shoulders in and nudged his horse into a trot, heading for town, as if he could escape Thorncress' questions by simply running away.

Thorncress came up beside him, his expression unreadable. "Mr. Loxley. What did you do?"

His neck ached where the creature had marked him, and the old scar on his fingertip throbbed as if it had been cut afresh. "I don't know. That thing said I belonged to it. Is that true? How can that be true if I don't—if I can't remember—"

"You're cursed."

Loxley flinched, casting his gaze away.

"You can't talk about it, can you? You remember little, and what you can recall, you can't tell me."

"I want to," Loxley said miserably, gripping the reins tightly. He wanted to crawl back into a warm bed and hide under the covers like a boy, and let Thorncress guard him from the things that crept in the dark—or he wanted to crawl into bed and take Thorncress with him, and wrap their limbs around one another like two drowning souls. He couldn't tell Thorncress that, either.

"Alright. I'll find it out some other way."

It was midnight, cold and dark and damp, and Loxley had flung them from their only shelter for the night. It was too late to seek other lodgings, and Loxley felt the night keenly. He hunched his shoulders against Thorncress' disappointment.

"I apologize," he said, directing his words to his horse's ears, which flicked back to listen. "I acted rashly. We should have stayed inside."

"We'll find some other place to sleep," Thorncress said, as if it didn't matter. "In the morning, we'll go to the town hall and find the records of sale for that house." His tone brooked no argument, which was comforting in its finality. "I will root out that creature's hold on you, Mr. Loxley."

The haw in his coat pocket weighed him down like a stone. "I wish I could be of more help."

"No matter. Such is the nature of faerie magic." Thorncress' gaze burned a hole between Loxley's shoulders. "I'll not leave you to its mercy, Mr. Loxley. I won't go unless you ask it of me."

Something in Loxley's chest eased at his words. "Thank you." His voice was barely more than a whisper, and he didn't know if Thorncress heard him. He couldn't imagine ever sending the man away, no matter the frustration that grew between them over Loxley's inability to speak of the hawthorn tree, its apple, or the marks the creature left on him.

Whether Thorncress heard him or not, he seemed to take Loxley's meaning, and they rode in silence for some time, letting their horses pick their way over the ground at an unhurried pace, leaving Pickering behind. As the town fell back, they passed an open field that stood silver in the moonlight, and Thorncress steered them to the side of the road.

"There's a barn ahead. We'll stop there to sleep."

"That's trespassing!" Loxley protested, though he followed Thorncress' lead all the same.

Thorncress either had a good eye for such things or he was led by some sixth sense, for the barn was empty, save for some stored farming equipment and a cat that, like them, had chosen the structure as its shelter. The cat was wary of them but made quick friends of the horses, and once the animals were settled, Thorncress made himself a bed in the hay as if it were a common occurrence to sleep in such a place.

Loxley hesitated, clinging to the edge of his coat.

"Have you never slept rough before, Mr. Loxley?" Thorncress asked, his amusement evident. "I must warn you, it's something you should get used to, if you're to travel with me a while yet."

"I can't say I make a habit of it," Loxley confessed, gingerly lowering himself to the barn floor. It was nothing more than hard-packed dirt, and cold without the hay. "Will we not freeze like this? The door barely closes! The drafts—"

"Come close to me," Thorncress interrupted, gesturing to the space beside him. "We've four walls and a roof. There are worse places to sleep."

Loxley inched closer, avoiding Thorncress' eyes as he finally lay down at the man's side, close enough to feel the warmth emanating from him, though not so close to touch. His face felt hot, and he prayed the dark would cover it.

"And the creature? Will it not find me here?"

Thorncress' expression darkened. "Sleep here, with me. If it returns, I'll fend it off, and if it comes into your dreams again, I'm near enough to hear you stir, and I'll wake you before it can drag you deeper into its enchantment."

Loxley's breath caught in his throat and he nodded, not daring to speak in case his voice gave away his desires. To sleep with him—they were sharing a bed after all, even if it was only made of hay, and though they were still wrapped in their coats, Loxley could feel Thorncress' body heat from across the bare inch of space between them.

Despite his earlier drowsiness, Loxley was keenly awake. The night air was crisp, gentled only by the sweet, musty scent of the hay and the nearby animals. Loxley wished he could see the stars. He had never slept outside before, but it struck him as romantic: to lay in a bed of heather and gaze up at the stars glittering above like some ancient, unreadable mosaic of the heavens. For one wild moment, he entertained the idea of travelling with Thorncress for weeks or months on end, riding through the north, following the roads by day and then sleeping under the stars, beholden to nothing and no one but each other.

Loxley tamped down the thought. He was still a slave to that creature's enchantment, and that alone would prevent him from ever travelling in such a manner, even if Thorncress desired such companionship. It was a romantic fantasy befitting a lovestruck youth more than a grown man, and Loxley blushed to have ever entertained it.

Thorncress turned to face him, propped up on one elbow. What little Loxley could see of his face, shadowed by his unkempt hair, looked thoughtful.

"What did you do, in London?"

"I was a scholar. A teacher, sometimes, though I preferred to be left to my own devices."

"What did you teach?"

"History, for the most part."

Thorncress' gaze was searching. "Folklore?"

"I touched on it here and there. It's impossible to tell a history of England without speaking of folklore now and again. The Arthurian legends alone . . . But I never talked much of Faerie, if that's what you mean. I was passingly familiar with the stories, but I'm sure I never drew any attention that way. I rarely gave any thought to Faerie at all, and when I did, it was very theoretical. A curiosity from the past that had little bearing on the present." Loxley twined a strand of straw between his fingers. "An error in judgement, obviously."

"A common one, though."

"But what of you? How did you come to learn of faerie magic? Your knowledge extends far beyond the common folklore, there's no denying it."

"I was raised with the certainty that Faerie was never more than a breath away. I could see it, sometimes, like another world plastered up against ours, shimmering behind the sky. On summer evenings I could hear bells ringing in the garden, though I knew better than to follow them."

Loxley's patchwork memories were full of biting frost and wicked teeth. "It sounds beautiful."

"Until you got too close." Thorncress fell silent for a moment. The barn creaked and moaned around them, the shifting of an old building in the night. "Ma was one of the Scottish Travellers," he said eventually. "One of the Lowland Roma. Da was a northern Englishman, and her people disowned her when she married him. I took after her, dark through and through, but my sister, she took after our Da's side. Lighter than you, even," he added, nodding to Loxley's wayward bronze curls. "Blonde as a summer's day, with red and gold showing through when the sun touched her hair just so."

"You must be lucky to have such a family," Loxley offered.

"Luck's a strange thing." Thorncress' gaze fell away. "Ma taught us all the old stories: Roma, Scottish, and Faerie alike, but knowledge cannot save you. Faerie takes without asking."

Swallowing, Loxley said softly, "I'm sorry."

Thorncress shook his head. "Go to sleep, Mr. Loxley. I'll keep you safe till dawn."

He turned away, signalling the end of the conversation, and Loxley obediently shut his eyes and waited for sleep to take him. But despite his efforts, he couldn't stop thinking of the way Thorncress' body was so close to his, emanating solid warmth, and how badly he wanted to curl into it, lay his head on Thorncress' chest, and find comfort in the steady beating of his heart.

Ashamed, he bit his lip until he tasted blood, and, focusing on that bitter pain, he turned onto his side to face away from Thorncress, staring into the dark, lonely shadows of the barn until sleep finally crested over him like a wave once more.

✳ ✳ ✳

He woke only once, from a dream or a memory, to see the little barn cat standing near his feet, her back arched and her tail puffed out like a chimney brush, hissing at something pacing outside the door. Loxley struggled upright, panic surging from beneath the weight of his exhaustion, but Thorncress laid one heavy hand against his chest and pressed him back down.

"It's alright," Thorncress said in a low voice. "I laid charms on this place that will hold till morning. Go back to sleep."

Loxley sank back down into his bed of hay, but he didn't shut his eyes until the shadow stopped moving back and forth under the doorframe. It was only when the cat stopped spitting that he relaxed, letting his eyes fall closed again as the cat lowered her tail and padded to his side, curling up in a ball against his knee, rumbling out a purr that reminded him, in his half-conscious state, of Thorncress.

※ ※ ※

The rest of the night passed without incident, and Thorncress roused him before dawn, one hand on his shoulder to draw him back to wakefulness. Loxley was stiff from sleeping on the floor, and his bones ached from the cold. Though Thorncress had remained a warm presence at his back throughout the night, it hadn't been enough to ward off the chill entirely. Used to sleeping in soft beds, Loxley felt the discomfort sharply. It would be just his luck to catch ill from a poor night's sleep—though Thorncress seemed wholly unaffected by it.

"We'll find somewhere to eat, then return to town to check the records of that house," he said, tending to his horse.

Like Thorncress, the animals were no worse for wear from spending the night in the old barn, and the horses whuffled their morning greetings gently into Thorncress' hair. The cat watched them from her place curled up in the saddle, and though she showed no inclination to approach them, neither did she shy away.

"You're a good cat," Loxley informed her, readying his horse.

The cat stared at him with round, golden eyes, unblinking, before turning away to wash her face. Dismissed, they led their horses from the barn and into the grey, pre-dawn dark, where they whiled away another hour before the town's businesses opened.

Following a somber breakfast during which neither of them were much inclined to conversation, they made their way to the town hall. They sat ensconced at a table in the back corner of the small library, Loxley with the record books and Thorncress leafing through the town's census, a frown sitting on his brow.

"We sold the house in 1795—I was twelve, then. The family who bought it from us sold it again one year later," Loxley read. He would have guessed he'd been younger; twelve was old enough that he should have built firmer memories of the time. "There's no reason given, and no record of where they went after." He drummed his fingers over the page, frustration welling up. "After another two buyers who both sold within a year or two, it stood empty, falling into disrepair. Obviously, no one will buy it now, but when we lived there, it was sound."

"Something drove them off. Look to the beginning. Who built the place?"

Loxley traced the line back up the page, hunting down the house's origins. "Built in 1708, by the Cobbs."

Thorncress hm'd and flicked through the pages of his census book. "Lots of Cobbs. Here's a Thomas and Anna Cobb at that address. They lived there till his death in 1782, when she moved in with her younger sister until she died three years later. Your parents bought the house from her."

"How did they die?"

"Old age, nothing remarkable." Thorncress took a closer look. "No— Very old age: he to a hundred, and she to a hundred and three."

"Children?"

He scanned the page, following the Cobb's lineage, then shook his head. "There's one mentioned in 1709, listed only as Baby Cobb, nothing more."

Loxley slumped. "A stillborn, most likely."

"Perhaps. Or, that's your changeling, swapped out at birth."

"But if the changeling lived, shouldn't it be listed with a name?"

"Unless the parents recognized it as fae, and never added a name to the records." Thorncress flipped the census book shut. "There's someone we should see." Standing, he slipped back into his coat like a second skin, and Loxley hastened to join him. "If she's still alive, then she's the only soul I know whose knowledge of the Folk rivals my own."

"A friend, or a scholar?" Loxley hazarded, following Thorncress as they swept from the town hall.

Thorncress glanced back over his shoulder, his dark eyes unreadable. "A stolen child."

CHAPTER FIVE

GRACE BLACKBURN

"You mean to tell me," Loxley said, as they traversed the long road to the east coast, "that you know someone who has actually escaped from Faerie?"

The wind was brisk and cutting as it whipped the words from Loxley's mouth, and his knee jostled Thorncress' as he fought to keep their mounts side by side.

"Or the Folk returned her. It can't be said."

"But it is possible to come back."

"Nothing's done without a price."

"Speak plainly, sir."

Thorncress heaved a sigh. "She's the only soul I've ever heard to return from Faerie after being stolen, but she knows not how it happened. She has no memory of her life before her return, nor how much time passed while she was gone. And, despite all these missing pieces, she still knows more of Faerie than any other soul alive. So, if the nature of your enchantment prevents you from telling me certain details about your history with this creature, perhaps she will succeed in working them out where I have failed."

"You haven't failed in anything," Loxley began, but Thorncress cut him off with an abrupt shake of his head.

"I don't know how to break the curse that holds your tongue. If I could do that, you might have shaken the creature entirely by now. I know full well that I've failed you."

"You've told me often enough that I judge myself too harshly. I'd be dead three times over by now if it weren't for you, so I'll hear no more of your failures, sir."

Thorncress set his jaw, his countenance dark, but didn't argue. It didn't feel like a victory, but Loxley nodded decisively and pulled away, putting space between them. Overhead, a storm was brewing in the clouds, turning them purple and blue like a bruise, heavy with unshed rain.

"We should take shelter before that breaks."

Even as the words left Thorncress' lips, the first raindrops splattered onto the road and over Loxley's face. He flinched as they hit, bursting fat and cold on his skin. As if the storm had only been waiting for its first messengers to land, the heavens opened all at once and flooded down. Loxley was soaked in seconds, his hair plastered to his face as the wind picked up, nipping at his cheeks as it sought some way under his coat to blow straight through his bones. Hunching his shoulders, he looked to Thorncress for direction.

They were still miles from their destination of Scarborough, and their journey would take longer still in the rain. There wasn't even an abandoned barn to take shelter in this time, or at least, not so far as Loxley could see. Still, Thorncress turned his horse from the road to head across the field that bordered it, and, biting back a curse, Loxley followed him.

At the far end of the field stood a sullen copse of trees, huddled against a crooked stone wall as if they, too, were seeking shelter from the storm. Thorncress rode for them unerringly, following the line of the wall until he came upon a gentle hollow in the ground, at which point he dismounted, and tethered his horse to a tree. Loxley followed behind, mirroring his actions in silence.

Thorncress didn't look at him. "This will do."

"We're going to sit in a ditch until the rain passes?"

Thorncress hunkered down with his back to the wall, drawing his hat low over his face. The wall was only four or five feet tall, but it cut the wind and even some of the driving rain. The horses edged close to it, their heads down, and reluctantly, Loxley followed suit.

They sat side by side, their arms around their knees and their collars drawn high, as they waited for the weather to break. The ground was cold, the rain colder, and Loxley couldn't recall the last time he had been so acutely miserable in his life. He wanted desperately to blame someone for his predicament, but his options were limited to Thorncress or himself. Thorncress had been nothing but generous—patient and steadfast when it would have been far easier to abandon Loxley to his fate—which meant, horribly, that Loxley must be the one at fault. Burying his hands in his pockets, he curled his fingers around the haw apple and wished he could remember the circumstance that had brought it into his possession. More than that, he wished he could simply pull his hand out and drop the thing into Thorncress' lap, and say—*I don't know why I have this or why it's so important, but please, get rid of it for me.*

He doubted breaking the enchantment would be so simple, but at least it would let him feel in charge of his own life, if only for a moment.

Instead, he withdrew his empty hand, and tucked them both under his arms, hugging himself as he shuffled over to lean into Thorncress' side. He was shivering, his teeth chattering helplessly as the rain soaked into his trousers, but there was nothing for it. The wall offered them the best protection they would find for miles, and he could think of nothing worse than getting back astride his horse to trudge on through the storm without any shelter at all. The horses seemed to agree, for whatever that was worth, and Thorncress—

He acknowledged Loxley's presence with a grunt, extending one arm to put around Loxley's shoulders and bring him closer still, until they were plastered against one another. The warmth was an immediate relief, and Loxley shoved his shame aside in order to work his hands under Thorncress' coat, holding them against his sides where it was warmest. Biting his lip, he put his shaking down to the cold, and nothing more.

To his credit, Thorncress didn't push him away, or indeed, even comment on the matter. "Rain like this won't keep up for long. It'll blow itself out soon enough."

Loxley made a shivering sound of agreement and tucked himself closer, daring to press his face to Thorncress' collar. The grip around his shoulders tightened for a second, and he braced himself to pull away before Thorncress could reject him, but it never happened. Gradually, Loxley relaxed. He was allowed this, if nothing more—a respite granted by the terrible weather and excused by the cold. Once the storm passed, he would withdraw, as was proper, and bury all his longings back in the depths of his soul, where they belonged. Thorncress needn't be troubled by them.

Gradually, the gales drove the clouds on to torment other places, and the rain lightened enough for Loxley to peer into the sky. The stark blues and violets of the storm were fading, replaced by the familiar wash of grey, even if it was darker than usual. Loxley knew on a rational level that they had hours left of daylight, but the sky had an odd cast to it that could have placed it anywhere between late afternoon and dusk.

"I've never felt quite so insignificant as I do under these skies," he said wistfully. "Certainly not in London, but even as a boy— They just stretch on forever, don't they?"

"There's a savage kind of beauty to it. Like looking over the edge of the world."

It felt different in the north, like the sky was closer to the earth, and so much bigger—or perhaps he was smaller, a dust speck amid the endless moors, and when he died, his body would return to the soil and the roots and he would be forgotten. The memory of being buried in the cold ground surfaced to the forefront of his thoughts. He had been comfortable, there—or had he only been so exhausted that he had mistaken the rest for comfort? Had he succumbed, and had Thorncress not arrived in time, the earth would have moved on, spinning in its slow rotation around the sun, as if he had never existed at all.

He didn't know whether he liked the idea.

Looking into the sky, he tried to see past the clouds. They were gradually thinning out, leaving the sky a flat, uniform grey: almost blue, with streaks of darker clouds near the horizon, like rough brush strokes.

"The borders are thinner here, between the worlds," Thorncress said. "Can you see it, behind the sky?"

"I can see something, sometimes," Loxley confessed, "or, rather, the idea of something. But I can't seem to put it into words. It's like an afterimage that I can see behind my eyelids, but I don't understand . . . What am I looking for?"

"Faerie."

An eerie wail flared up, haunting as a ghost, and they both froze.

"What—" Loxley began, but Thorncress pressed him back against the wall, one gloved hand held firmly over Loxley's face. Blinded, Loxley froze, his breath caught in his chest.

"Hush," Thorncress breathed, his voice low in Loxley's ear. "Keep your eyes shut."

The cry grew louder, wavering as it danced through the sky. Like the howling of long-gone wolves or the musical baying of dogs at hunt, the sound was ancient and predatory and terribly lonesome. Loxley shivered in his skin and turned closer to Thorncress like he could crawl inside the man's coat.

"What is it?"

"Faerie hounds."

It was said that the hounds were great white beasts, thick-furred and pale-eyed, creatures that seemed lit from within with some unearthly fire. Soundless when they ran, save for the baying that lifted from their throats like a cry to heaven. A death omen to all who looked on them, still said to roam the Highlands, but long vanished from fair England. Their song pierced Loxley to his core, filling him with such primal terror that he could do nothing but bury his face in Thorncress' throat, shaking—

Yet it tugged at him, too, calling for him to lift his head and see the beasts that could make such a sound. They must be beautiful. They must be—

"Hold still." One hand, Thorncress kept wrapped over Loxley's eyes; the other, he buried in Loxley's hair, holding his head down against Thorncress' chest so he couldn't give in to that awful temptation and look. "They will pass us soon."

Loxley's heart gave a sickening lurch. "Do you see them? You must cover your eyes, as well!"

"I cannot see them. They're not so near as that."

"How can you be sure—"

"I know their sounds. Their cries carry a fair distance. They will pass us by, and we'll be left unharmed. But keep your eyes shut, all the same."

Gradually, the cries faded, as Thorncress promised. Neither of them moved until silence rang out across the moors, strangely oppressive in contrast to the sharp clarity that the hounds had brought. Thorncress held him a moment longer before withdrawing his hands, sitting back to lean against the wall as he had done before.

Loxley stared up at the sky, watching his breath bloom in curls of damp frost, like his lungs were trying to build their own tiny clouds.

"You're alright," Thorncress said.

"You've heard the hounds before."

"A few times."

"Is it always like that?"

Thorncress glanced at him.

"Spiritual, almost." Loxley's gaze wandered the heavens. "Like how the most devout describe their religion, being connected to something so much bigger than yourself. Terrible and beautiful, all at once."

Thorncress exhaled in a plume of frost. "Yes. It's always like that."

"Are you a religious man, Mr. Thorncress?"

"I am. Or perhaps it's more accurate to say that I was. We were raised Catholic, but I've not set foot in a church for service for many years, now. And yourself?"

"I believe in God," Loxley said simply. "Though, I suppose it's telling that when I look at the sky, I'm searching not for heaven but for Faerie." He paused, and stillness hung between them for a moment. "Is it true, what happens if you see the hounds?"

"You die. On the third dawn." Abruptly restless, Thorncress rose, tearing himself from Loxley's side to straighten his coat and head for the horses. "We should leave now if we're to make Scarborough by nightfall. Come, Mr. Loxley. On your feet."

"Should we not give the hounds more time to clear the area?" Loxley asked, struggling upright with the help of the wall.

Thorncress swung into the saddle, settling there with an unreadable expression. "No need. They're not given to linger."

※ ※ ※

Scarborough was a fair-sized town situated by the North Sea, and Thorncress led them to the very edge of the coast, where a lone house stood on the cliff overlooking the water. A rowan tree grew in the front yard by the door, with cheerful red berries clinging to its branches, and an iron horseshoe hung above the entrance. The breeze was stiff as it blew in off the waves, and Loxley could taste the salt in the air.

"What's she like, your changeling?" he asked as they rode up to her gate. Her yard was an overgrown tangle of a garden, the plants all brown and bristly as winter fast approached, and the windows of her house were dark.

"Human."

Dismounting, Thorncress strode through the gate and up to the door without hesitation, knocking soundly before glancing back to see if Loxley was following. Loxley fixed his horse's reins out of the way before hurrying to join him.

The door eased open, and Thorncress smiled. "Hello, Grace. I've brought a visitor. Mr. Loxley, this is Ms. Grace Blackburn. Grace: William Loxley."

"A pleasure to meet you, Ms. Blackburn." Loxley stepped forward to offer his hand, only to realize at the last moment that Ms. Blackburn couldn't see him.

She was a handsome woman of Thorncress' age, or perhaps a few years older, her hair gone to silver and grey, and with capable, fine-boned hands, calloused from years of work. But it was her eyes that were most remarkable. The irises were clouded over like the pearlescent whites of opal stones, and her pupils were stranger still. For instead of being a single circle, there were two, conjoined in the center of each pale iris to make a new shape, twice the size as they should have been.

Loxley caught himself staring, and though she was obviously blind, he quickly flushed and looked away, clasping his hands behind his back, ashamed of his poor manners.

"I hope we find you well," Thorncress said.

"I'm yet among the living," she replied lightly. "What can I do for you gentlemen? It's been a while since you paid me a visit, and I take it this isn't a social call."

"Mr. Loxley has need of your expertise. Faerie's after him," Thorncress supplied, in his usual blunt manner. "A grown changeling, is my bet. They're bound together, though I've had no luck uncovering the root of it."

She turned her sightless gaze on Loxley. "Is that true indeed, Mr. Loxley? It's not many men who attract the Folk's attention in this day and age."

"I have no explanation for it, except that I must be cursed with singularly bad luck."

"Bad luck's rarely without a cause. Come inside, the two of you, and let's work out what's to be done."

The inside of the house was aglow with a small fire crackling in the hearth, though otherwise unlit. Plain rugs covered the wooden floors, and the kitchen counters and cupboards were neatly organized, lined with jars of preserves and dried goods, and bundled herbs hung from the naked rafters alongside pots and pans, just above one's head, within easy reach. It was a cozy, well-lived-in little home, and one that put Loxley instantly at ease. As Ms. Blackburn put the kettle on and pressed a hot meal on them—chicken stew, and a loaf of thick-sliced brown bread, baked fresh that morning—the three of them settled around the kitchen table, and Thorncress told her their tale. Loxley added certain details here and there, embellishing where Thorncress was missing pieces of the story, though he could only offer so much. He made no mention of the hawthorn apple, nor could he speak of the creature's testimony that they had once played together when he was a child. Ms. Blackburn gazed at him, or rather through him, her brow furrowed thoughtfully, but she didn't interrupt except to ask for occasional clarification.

"So, there you have it," Loxley said when they reached the end. Their bowls had been emptied, and they held their mugs of tea close to their chests as the steam wafted in lazy ribbons to the rafters. "Mr. Thorncress suggested that you could perhaps shed some light on the matter, and I know not where else to turn."

"It's an interesting story, and a problem not easily solved. I hope he didn't promise any miracles from me."

Thorncress glanced darkly at Loxley. "I've been upfront with him."

"It's true. I know the chance of my escaping such a situation is slim, but—do you think there's any hope for me at all?"

"There's always hope," Ms. Blackburn said, though she didn't elaborate. Instead, turning to Thorncress, she said, "If you're staying the night, you ought stable the horses in town. I'll keep Mr. Loxley in good company till you're back."

Thorncress rose, nodding to Loxley, and departed without a word. Loxley watched him go with some consternation. They had not been parted in days, except for Loxley's dreams, and it roused an uncomfortable sensation of anxiety in the pit of his stomach to be without his companion. He had been content, not so long ago, to be left alone with his books and papers. How quickly his life had changed.

"Now that we're alone, perhaps you can speak more freely."

Loxley turned back to face his hostess, cradling his tea. She gazed calmly in his direction, her twin pupils swimming over his face without ever sharpening into focus.

"I know the enchantment has your tongue. There are things you can't say in front of him, no matter how badly you might wish to."

"I don't think I can say them at all."

"You might find me an exception to the rule. Faerie magic often does, for better or for worse. Do you know the cause of your enchantment?"

"No," said Loxley, unhappily.

"But you know more than you've told Mr. Thorncress."

"I have no answers, only clues, and when I try to speak of them, I choke on the words. It's like being asked to share a secret so personal that my whole being shies away from the prospect, and try as I might to overcome it, I can't bring myself to tell him—" He snapped his mouth shut abruptly. There were other secrets he was keeping from Thorncress besides those relating to the creature, and they needed to be kept from Ms. Blackburn, as well.

"What can't you tell him?"

Silently, he reached into his coat pocket and curled his fingers around the haw, drawing it out and letting it sit in the palm of his hand. It was such a little thing, smooth and round with its dark red skin, as hard as a stone. He held his breath as he rolled it back and forth between his hands. There was an element of risk, handling it out in the open where anyone might recognize it for the strange, fae totem it must be, but Ms. Blackburn saw and said nothing, merely gazing through him, until Loxley drew a shuddering breath and slipped it back into his pocket.

"Mr. Thorncress says you were stolen as a child," he said, in a rush of exhalation. "Forgive my rudeness, but is it true?"

"If it is, then my story begs even more questions than yours. I don't mind telling it, but if it's reassurance you're looking for, you'll not find it here."

"Not reassurance, but perhaps understanding? Though I suspect even that is beyond me."

"I don't believe the Folk are wholly beyond our understanding," Ms. Blackburn said slowly. "Inhuman as they are, they do operate by a certain set of rules that we can predict—to some extent, at least. The trouble is that people are quick to forget them."

"Did you find some loophole by which you were able to escape Faerie, after being stolen away?"

"I don't know. I have no memory of that land whatsoever, nor my life before it. Whether they stole me as a babe and I grew to adulthood in Faerie, or they stole me as a young woman, I can't say. Neither can I guess how long I spent there. I tell people that my birth date is 1765, but I could have been born a hundred years ago, or a thousand. My memories begin in a farmer's field, where I woke beneath a hawthorn tree one dawn."

Loxley stilled, his tea raised halfway to his mouth.

"I had nothing but the clothes on my back, ragged and worn as if they had been passed down through generations. I didn't even have a name. I was perhaps twenty years old, though I had no way of knowing my exact age. To this day, I don't know it. But I made my way to Scarborough town, where I eventually settled."

"There are injuries that can lead to such amnesia," Loxley said carefully.

"Aye, to be sure. I spent a fair time travelling in those days, going from town to town, looking for anyone who could recognize me. But no one ever did. From Scotland to London I went, and not a soul could put a name to my face." She raised one hand as if sensing Loxley's restlessness. "Does it prove I had come from Faerie? Not at all. Perhaps I preferred the idea of Faerie rather than one of foul play. But the magic of that place marks you, as I think you well know. It lingers long after you've forgotten what caused it."

"And you have no memory of Faerie whatsoever?" Loxley didn't know whether to be disappointed or relieved. There was no tale of Faerie from which he could draw reassurance, but the thought of being drawn into such an unknown place sent dread coiling through him.

Ms. Blackburn hesitated. "Not of the land itself, no. But I have a recurring dream where I'm walking through a field towards a forest, and with every step, the earth shifts under me, like I'm wading through tall grass, and the soil is so soft that I'm sinking. Everything is rolling around me, like the planet is turning faster than I can move, and the stars are spinning like coins in the sky. It's a feeling of terrible anticipation, but I always wake up before I reach the woods." She shook her head. "I don't know if it's real. I don't know what would happen if I reached the trees. I only know that when I wake, it's the loneliest, most terrible feeling in the world."

"I'm sorry," Loxley said helplessly.

She smiled crookedly and shrugged. "Such is our lot, the fae-touched. We may carve out some semblance of normalcy after they've lost interest in us, but Faerie will only ever be a hair's-breadth away, ever just beyond our reach."

"Do you want to reach it?" Loxley asked with morbid curiosity. "Is it not better for them to have lost interest in you?"

She studied him, her eyes silver in the firelight. "Are you a religious man, Mr. Loxley?" Her question echoed his, from hours earlier.

"I try to be."

"If you knew the touch of God, only for an instant, would you not give anything to feel His touch again? Even if it burned you?"

Loxley bit his tongue. It was far easier to believe in Faerie than in God, of late, and to compare the two was blasphemy. The steam from their tea curled between them like a serpent.

"It's not all bad," Ms. Blackburn said in a softer tone, when he made no reply. "I've met people born blind, and they experience their dreams just as they experience their waking world, all in darkness. Perhaps I was born sighted, then, and only lost it after I returned. If it's the only clue I have to my past life, before I woke in that strange field, then I'll take it."

"You woke under a hawthorn tree."

"As did you, in the moors."

"There's one in my yard, as well," Loxley said quickly, before the words could choke him. "I used to play under it, as a boy. There's something about it that I don't want— That I can't have Mr. Thorncress knowing, but I can't—"

He choked on his tongue and fell to gasping, his knuckles clenched white against the table's edge.

When he had regained his breath, Ms. Blackburn asked, "Can you write it down, rather than try to speak?" She withdrew a stub of chalk from her pocket, offering it to him across the table.

"Even if I can, you won't be able to read it."

She held the chalk out impassively. "Try."

He took the chalk, curling it between his thumb and fingers as he lowered it to the tabletop. He tried to form a sentence in his mind: *I have an apple from that tree on me at all times, and I don't know why.* But as soon as he touched the tip of the chalk to the wood, his hand began to shake uncontrollably, and his head filled with a terrible roar that hurt so badly, it blacked out his vision. Gritting his teeth, he forced his hand to write two words before he dropped the chalk quite against his will, and collapsed back into his chair.

Crooked white letters stared up at him from the table. He had written THE APPLE, and no more.

"I can't manage it." He swallowed a shaky draught of his tea. "The tree is at the heart of it, I'm certain, but I can't . . ."

Miserably, he held out the chalk for her to take, and she accepted it with a thoughtful hum.

"They're said to be gateways between the worlds. A lonesome hawthorn tree, standing all alone in a field, is something to be avoided. Farmers won't cut them down, even if they have to plough their fields or build their roads around them. Hawthorn for the fae, and rowan to protect against them."

Loxley slipped his hand back into his pocket, almost unconsciously. "Does their presence leave you more vulnerable to the Folk?"

"Seeking them out may be seen as an invitation, of sorts. But if the Folk want to find you, they will, hawthorn tree or no."

Loxley clenched his fingers around the haw. "Did you ever wonder if you yourself might be one of them?"

A heavy step sounded outside the door an instant before Thorncress opened it, and Loxley withdrew his hand from his pocket so quickly that he jostled his tea, spilling it over himself.

CHAPTER SIX

THE CHANGELING TEST

Thorncress glanced between the two of them. "Apologies. I didn't mean to startle you."

"I heard you coming," Ms. Blackburn said, "but it seems that Mr. Loxley's ears are not so keen."

"Clumsy." Loxley set his mug down on the kitchen table as he swept his sleeve over the chalk letters, obscuring the words and hating himself for it. "I must have been too deep in thought to pay attention."

"I trust the roads were good?" Ms. Blackburn asked.

"Still a mess from the rain, but it's not dark yet, so I've travelled through worse."

"And you didn't encounter any trouble?" Loxley asked.

"What trouble did you anticipate between my house and the town stable?" Ms. Blackburn asked, seeming amused.

"We heard the faerie hounds earlier. I don't know if they'd come so close to town, but better safe than sorry."

Her features sharpened as she turned her head in Thorncress' direction. "Reckless—" she hissed, but he interrupted her with a short sound of negation.

"We didn't seek them out."

"Of course not," Loxley said, faintly baffled. "You can't seek out a death omen: they go where they will."

"Not an omen but a cause," Thorncress said flatly. "Else any soul on the brink of death should see them. It's not the case."

Loxley waved his words aside. "In any case: no man would seek them out. I'm only grateful that Mr. Thorncress recognized the sound and was quick enough to shield me from my own curiosity."

"You should be more careful," Ms. Blackburn told Thorncress sternly. "If not for your sake, then for his."

"I am being careful. As he says: the hounds go where they will."

Tension hung heavily between them, marring the comfort of the little home, until Loxley cleared his throat, picking up his mug just to set it down again.

"I trust you had a productive conversation while I was away," Thorncress finally said.

"I can't say how productive it was. I could scarcely tell her any more than I could tell you."

"But he raised one question that I can answer, if nothing else," Ms. Blackburn said. "If he's not human, we can tell."

Thorncress slowly turned to regard Loxley with narrowed eyes. "And why should you not be human?"

"You asked me if I had any siblings who might have been replaced by fae children. But what if I myself am a changeling?"

"Do you have reason to suspect that?"

Loxley bit the inside of his cheek to keep from blurting out his secret. "I don't know. Only—sometimes, my thoughts—they become un-Christian, you see, and I wondered . . ."

Thorncress' gaze gentled. "Any man can have un-Christian thoughts from time to time, Mr. Loxley. It doesn't make him a monster, and it doesn't make him fae."

Loxley looked away, burning with shame. "Even so. I should like to be sure."

"It's simple enough to test," said Ms. Blackburn. "If it will put your mind at ease, then by all means, let's see the manner of your nature."

She rose and crossed the little kitchen to the wall of cabinets, opening one unerringly and withdrawing a small, carved wooden box, which she set down on the table between them.

"Inside is a charmed piece of cold iron. The Fair Folk cannot touch it without being terribly burned, but any human untouched by Faerie can handle it without harm." Lifting the latch and opening the lid, Ms. Blackburn smiled mirthlessly. "For those of us who have been touched, the effect will be unpleasant, but far from deadly."

Loxley's fingers twitched restlessly on the tabletop. "Then, if I am a changeling, this test could kill me?"

"Unlikely. You may lose a few fingers." Her sightless eyes stared into his. "But none of us believe you're one of them, Mr. Loxley. Still." She pushed the box towards him. "It's your choice."

He swallowed, dry-throated.

"Here." Thorncress lifted the charm out. It was a pretty little thing, polished to a silver shine, and made in the shape of an intricately knotted cross. It rested heavily in his palm, looking like nothing more than a piece of lovingly crafted jewelry. Thorncress lifted it between two fingers, showing Loxley the red mark it left behind.

"Did it burn you?" Loxley asked anxiously.

He shook his head. "It's reacting to the magic on me. I've dealt with Faerie enough times over the years that it clings to me like a second skin. This has barely singed me, and the mark will fade in a moment." He held the charm out to Ms. Blackburn, waiting patiently until she took it.

A faint hiss of steam rose from her skin when she touched it, and Loxley flinched, but it quickly settled.

"I spent years burning Faerie away from me," she said, turning the charm thoughtfully between her hands. "It took a long time, and it's still not completely gone. It never will be." She held out her palm for Loxley to see. A scorch mark lay in the center of her hand, raised and painful looking, but she seemed unbothered. "Faerie dug in too deep for me to ever shake it entirely. But this charm cannot hurt me the way it would one of the true Folk." She held it out to him, expectantly. "This is but a superficial burn, and I've had worse hurts in my life. I expect I will again."

Loxley hesitated, one hand outstretched to take the charm, his fingers stopping just short of actually touching it.

"You're not a changeling, Mr. Loxley," Thorncress said.

"How can you be sure?"

"I know them," he replied simply. "None of the Folk can hide their true nature so well, not even those raised in the human world. Their minds are too alien for it." He placed one hand under Loxley's, a solid, steady presence that acted as an anchor—not holding him in place, but reassuring him of support.

Taking a deep breath, Loxley took the charm from Ms. Blackburn's hand.

It burned.

The pain was startling, a sudden flare of freezing cold against his skin, and he swore and dropped it, clattering over the tabletop. Frowning, Thorncress caught his hand and raised it. The tip of the index finger was tinged black, as if frostbitten, with only the slender scar showing through white.

"What happened?" Ms. Blackburn asked.

"It burned him." Thorncress retrieved the charm without releasing Loxley's hand.

"What—" Loxley began, his voice shaking, but Thorncress interrupted him with a shake of his head.

"Forgive me, Mr. Loxley, but we need a more definitive answer than that. You let go too soon."

"It burned me! Is that not answer enough?"

Putting aside the charm, Thorncress took Loxley's hand in both of his, and for one heart-stopping second, Loxley thought he meant to kiss it. But no—he only examined it, turning Loxley's hand this way and that before brushing his own fingers over Loxley's burn, and then finally letting him go. Loxley tucked his hand to his chest like the wing of a wounded bird, feeling far too vulnerable.

"It singed you, nothing more. It did no permanent damage, and you lost no skin. Now." Thorncress took up the charm again, gently pressing it into Loxley's shaking hand, and closing his fingers around it so Loxley had no chance to escape. "Hold it, and don't be afraid."

The metal burned him, or maybe it was only so cold that it felt like burning. He couldn't help his fear: the way his body trembled and his heart beat far too fast, but he didn't let go. Strengthened by Thorncress' hand covering his, he shut his eyes and took deep breaths, willing himself to calm.

"Alright."

Thorncress released him, and Loxley uncurled his fingers one by one. The charm glinted up from his palm; Thorncress plucked it out, revealing the skin beneath. It was red, as if the metal had been cold after all, but it lacked the darkness of the mark on his finger, or the burn that Ms. Blackburn had shown them. Tentatively stretching his hand out, Loxley tested the pain, and found there to be little. He had been more shocked than hurt, it seemed, and gradually, his heartbeat slowed to normal.

"You're not a changeling," Thorncress repeated.

"But the black mark—"

"Shows that Faerie magic has got under your skin, the same as it has us. It doesn't make you one of them."

Loxley nodded and folded his hands together, ashamed. To have hoped to pin his faults on Faerie! Such arrogance to think he could use that as an excuse. He was a man, as human and mortal as any other, and his thoughts and urges were his own.

"Thank you for your patience," he said in a small voice. "My fear had crowded out my reason."

"Don't apologize," said Ms. Blackburn. "There's much to fear. But tonight, at least, rest easy. You're safe within these walls."

"Ms. Blackburn has the best protected house in England. Nothing can come knocking at your window while you're here."

Loxley's breath rattled out in a sigh of relief. The thought of being properly safe for the first time since he had woken in that faerie ring made him weak and suddenly exhausted.

"Thank you for your hospitality, Ms. Blackburn. I know we arrived unexpectedly, and I hope we didn't put you to much trouble, but this is . . ." He cast about for the word to describe the enormity of what it meant to him. "A godsend."

Something wry flashed across her face, mirrored in Thorncress'—the irony of his word choice wasn't lost on Loxley, though he had nothing better to offer, godless as their situation was—before it settled into sympathetic warmth.

"You're welcome to stay as long as you need, Mr. Loxley. And I'm sure Mr. Thorncress has told you that his company is no intrusion on my peace."

"Still— Thank you."

Thorncress grunted. "Don't fret, Ms. Blackburn. Your hospitality is sincere, but we'll leave you be soon enough. A night or two, just long enough to get his feet back under him, and we'll be on our way."

She reached over to cuff his shoulder, her aim unfaltering. "Don't you listen to him, Mr. Loxley. It's no bother if you need to stay longer."

Loxley glanced uncertainly at Thorncress. It would be nice to rest a while, somewhere safe and sound beyond the creature's reach, if what he said of Ms. Blackburn's protections were true. But Thorncress was as restless as Loxley was given to earthly comforts, and he could see that the man was already planning the next leg of their journey.

He wouldn't argue against it. If Thorncress thought it best to keep moving until they learned of some way to break the creature's hold for good, then Loxley would follow him.

But staying in a house and a warm bed, a room to call his own, if only for a few days, was a tempting prospect.

"Well, sleep now, in any case. I've a spare room with a bed, and you're welcome to use it for as long as you need."

Loxley glanced at Thorncress. "I can think of nothing better than a night of uninterrupted sleep."

"You go on, Mr. Loxley," Ms. Blackburn said. "The two of us have things yet to discuss, I think."

Thorncress inclined his head. "As she says. Make yourself comfortable, Mr. Loxley. I'll join you later on."

The spare room was sparse but more serviceable than Loxley had expected, with a thick quilt on the bed, and the rowan tree just visible from the corner of the window. Though Loxley wanted nothing more than to lay down and give himself to sleep, his mind was restless.

He rolled the charm back and forth between his palms. It still felt cold, but merely the cold of metal in winter, not the burning, bone-deep chill it had borne at his first touch. It didn't hurt him at all, save for when he touched it to that scar, where it ached and turned his skin black.

He'd had that scar for as long as he could remember. Had the creature marked him so young? He had no memory of it, but why else would it react to the charm in such a way? With a sick sense of fascination, he held the charm against his fingertip, biting his tongue as the burn cut straight through him, sending a numb agony shooting through his hand and up his arm, all the way to his heart, as if he had struck a nerve. When he could bear it no longer, he dropped the charm with a shaken curse, immediately wrapping his hurt finger up in his other hand and holding it close to him, trying to coax some warmth back into it.

He had blackened his skin up to the first knuckle, his nail blue as a bruise. Beneath the black, the scar remained, a thin line that refused to be burned away.

Whatever magic had cursed him there, it was too old and too settled in his flesh for the charm to work out.

Unconsciously, his fingers moved to the side of his neck. He didn't need to see that the mark was still there; he could feel it, as surely as if the creature had its teeth in him still. Carefully, he knelt to retrieve the charm. Such an innocuous little thing when he held it in his palm: no more than a trinket, it seemed. But it held a power to rival faerie magic, and that couldn't be discounted.

The mark on his neck was new, compared to the scar on his finger. He couldn't burn away the scar, but the bruise—

Slowly, he raised the charm to the side of his throat, and held it above his skin for a second, sick with anticipation. It was going to hurt, but he wasn't afraid of the pain. He was only afraid that it would be for nothing.

Shutting his eyes, he pressed the charm to his skin in a single decisive moment, clenching his jaw against the immediate agony. It felt as if he were burning away his flesh with a branding iron, so overpowering that it was almost unbearable, but he hated the thought of being stuck with that mark more than he hated suffering for it. He held fast even as his knees gave out and he crumpled to the floor, his vision sparking red and his nerves screaming. He held it until the pain was so all-encompassing that it stopped registering as pain at all, and he wondered, numbly and in shock, at the strange bodily experience of it. He held it until his fingers finally lost their grip and the charm fell to the rug at his side, landing with a dull thump like a common bauble, and he could do nothing but stare after it.

He didn't know how long he sat like that. Logically, it must have been mere minutes, for no one came to check on him, but time slipped away, and it could have been hours. When he finally came back to himself, it was like waking from a daze. His thoughts cleared incrementally, and sensation returned to his body: the feeling of the floor, hard under his knees; the cramp in his hand from holding the charm for so long; and finally, only after the rest had come back, did the pain in his neck flare to life.

Wincing, he rose to his knees and struggled upright, gripping the edge of the bed to pull himself to his feet. Ms. Blackburn had no mirrors in her home, having little use for them, but Loxley made his way to the darkened window to study his reflection in the glass.

The skin of his neck was black, as he had expected: rough and blistering in places, like a terrible sunburn, layers of it already peeling away. Gingerly, he raised one hand to touch it, and immediately flinched back from the pain. There was no way to tell if the bruise beneath had been burned away, but surely it must have been. The bruise was only a surface mark, after all. In a few days, the burn would peel, and take the faerie mark away with it.

Satisfied, Loxley tucked the charm into his trouser pocket and shed his boots. As long as he left the door open, the fire's warmth would reach the bed, though he hesitated before removing his coat. He wanted the warmth, but more importantly, he wanted to hide the damage he had done to himself. Compromising, he discarded the coat and wound his scarf back around his neck. Checking his reflection once more and assured that the scarf hid the burn entirely, he climbed into bed and willed himself to sleep.

But it was the first night that Thorncress wasn't within arm's reach, and though Loxley believed that Ms. Blackburn's house was well defended, it was too easy to imagine the creature lurking just below the window, reaching its long fingers up to the glass.

Taking a deep breath, Loxley turned onto his side, putting his back to the window, and concentrated instead on the gentle sound of conversation that drifted in from the kitchen. Thorncress and Ms. Blackburn had been talking for some time, it seemed, and Loxley stared out into the darkened corridor, letting their words wash over him.

"Are you really going to spend the rest of your life chasing after her?" Ms. Blackburn asked.

"I made her a promise."

"And there's no soul on this earth can say you've not done your damnedest to keep it. But you're killing yourself, John."

Thorncress huffed mirthlessly. "Not yet, I'm not."

"She wouldn't want this."

"Well, she's not here to tell me so herself, is she?"

They fell silent for a moment.

"What of him, then?" she finally asked. "If you can't break the enchantment, will you take that as a personal failing, too?"

"Yes," said Thorncress bluntly.

"Oh, John."

Her voice was so sad that Loxley shifted instinctively, as if he could rise from the bed to offer some broken comfort to her—to them both—but they stilled and went silent at the sound. Loxley froze, his heart rabbiting, as he waited to hear whether they would continue their conversation.

"You should get some sleep," Thorncress said eventually, accompanied by the sound of him rising. "We both should."

"Aye." She sounded disappointed. "Good night, John."

"Good night, Grace."

Loxley feigned sleep as Thorncress came into the room, shedding his outermost layers before pausing at the edge of the bed. Loxley wondered if Thorncress was going to take a chair again, but there were none in the room. He would have to sleep in the kitchen, by the fire—unless he slept with Ms. Blackburn. But though they shared a history, they didn't seem so inclined, as far as Loxley could tell.

"Loxley? Are you awake?"

Loxley stirred, turning to blink up at him. "Are you sleeping here tonight?"

"I don't have to."

Loxley blew out a sigh of exasperated relief. That, at least, was familiar ground. "Don't be ridiculous. Even you cannot sleep comfortably in a kitchen chair."

"I could," Thorncress retorted, though he didn't argue any further than that as he relegated his coat and boots to a neat pile on the floor, and himself to the side of the bed nearest the window.

"It's too cold for that nonsense," Loxley said, carefully keeping his back turned as Thorncress stripped down to his underclothes. "I'd have been glad to have your warmth days ago."

"Sorry to have kept you waiting. I hadn't realized I was meant to serve as your personal hearth."

Loxley drew back the covers, leaving room for Thorncress to slip between them, keeping his gaze trained on the doorway, where it was safe. "No reason for us both to go cold. The bed is large enough to share." It was, but only in the strictest sense of the word. Two grown men would make a tight fit, and Loxley was a fool for putting himself in such a position, but his point still stood. It was cold and getting colder every night, and the fireplace was in another room.

"I had thought you might take the opportunity for some space," Thorncress said carefully. "We've had nought but each other's company for days."

"I wouldn't offer if I—" Loxley cut himself short. "I would rather have your company than my own. Besides which, it's not fair that you should sleep in a chair each night while I take every bed for myself, especially when there is room enough for two."

"Very well. If you should change your mind, only let me know, and I'll do just fine on the floor."

"You're hardly some ruffian I met on the roadside, sir. We're more than well enough acquainted to share a bed for the night." In a more somber tone, Loxley added, "And I've grown used to having you at my side. Though I don't doubt Ms. Blackburn's wards, I should feel better with you near."

Thorncress finally took to the bed. The mattress shifted as he climbed in, and he adjusted the covers over them both before settling in against the pillow. He emanated heat, a solid presence that Loxley didn't dare look upon, shielding him from whatever lurked beyond the windowpanes.

"Do you not get lonely," Loxley asked, his gaze wandering the dark shape of the doorframe, "roaming the north as you do? I used to be content to keep my own company, but even then, I had colleagues and fellow boarders and the like. London is a far cry from York."

"I prefer the loneliness of solitude to that which I find amongst others," Thorncress said eventually. "People don't take kindly to my looks. They'll cross the street to avoid me, call me Gypsy and take me for a liar and a thief, whether they've spoken two words to me or no. I'd rather the company of the hills and dales."

A fierce anger flared in Loxley's breast, and he turned over to find Thorncress in the dark. "It's not right that they should treat you so."

"No," Thorncress agreed drily, "it's not."

Embarrassed, Loxley asked in a quieter tone, "Would you not go to live with your mother's people?"

Thorncress shook his head. "I've never met them. I don't belong there any more than I belong in London."

"I'm sorry." Loxley laid a tentative hand on Thorncress' shoulder. "For what it's worth, I've never seen you as either a liar or a cheat. I believe you to be the most honest, steadfast man I've ever met."

Thorncress was silent for a moment, and Loxley withdrew his touch, fearing that he had overshot his mark. But then Thorncress said, "If they judge me too poorly, I fear you put me in too fair a light."

"I don't think I do."

If that was a smile curling in the corner of Thorncress' mouth, it was too dark for Loxley to be certain of it.

"I appreciate that, even if you're mistaken. Good night, Mr. Loxley."

Loxley didn't wish their talk to end so soon. He wanted to sit up and question Thorncress about his earlier conversation with Ms. Blackburn, but couldn't think of a way to do it without admitting he had been eavesdropping. He wanted to trace the shape of Thorncress' face with his fingertips, the dark sweep of his eyelashes, the line of his nose, the bow of his lips, and make him understand the extent of Loxley's esteem for him. If he could, he would erase every cruel word and unkind look Thorncress had collected over the years and replace them with his own whispered affirmations, even if Thorncress didn't believe them.

But he could do none of those things.

He tucked his hands under the pillow and shut his eyes.

"Good night, Mr. Thorncress."

CHAPTER SEVEN

UNNATURAL ACTS

One night at Grace Blackburn's house turned into two, which became a week. She and Thorncress spent hours each day with their heads bent together, poring over magical theories and charms as they sought to break Loxley's enchantment. Loxley himself spent the days baking bread under Ms. Blackburn's tutelage, wandering the town during the daylight hours, or tending to the long-neglected garden. Sometimes he walked to the edge of the cliff to look out over the sea, and watch its cold, dark waters crash against the beach far below.

He might have spent hours there, admiring the brutality of the waves and breathing in the sharp salt air, were it not so cold. It rained more often than not, and the sky seemed low enough to touch.

But despite the weather, he felt quite safe exploring the outdoors as long as it was light, and true to Thorncress' promise, the house was as a fortress against the creature, provided Loxley was ensconced within its walls come dusk. It was then that he reapplied the charm to his fae marks, the bruise and the scar, in the effort to burn them away entirely. The pain lessened as his body adjusted to the ritual, but he could never be sure whether the marks were lessening as well.

He could still hear the creature pacing the perimeter after dark, hissing curses to the stars, but he never saw it from the windows, and his dreams were empty. He might have found it lonely, were it not for Thorncress' presence at his side.

For Thorncress was the most exquisitely torturous distraction.

Loxley had not fully relaxed in his presence, but they had come to an unspoken understanding as bedmates. Loxley was always careful to fall asleep on his side, his face turned to the door and with a respectable distance between them—or, as respectable as could be had in so small a bed. But if they woke much closer—if they woke with limbs entangled, or with Loxley's hand upon Thorncress' chest, or with Thorncress' arm draped carelessly over Loxley's waist—neither of them mentioned it, disengaging and parting ways as if nothing had happened at all.

Loxley cherished those tender, waking moments as much as he despaired of them. He had never been so taken with a man. When his thoughts were not occupied with Faerie, they turned to Thorncress: to his reserved mannerisms, his blunt speech, the fall of his hair in his face. The elegance of his hands and the dedication with which he tended his horse, the furrow of his brow as he sought to concoct some plan to save Loxley's soul.

Never had Loxley fallen so hard, nor so fast. He was dependent on the man—he knew that. But while Thorncress was plainly frustrated with his inability to break the enchantment, he showed no sign of impatience with Loxley beyond that, no matter how Loxley clung to him. It filled Loxley with a little curl of warmth to think that perhaps Thorncress was equally fond of him, though he never dared to hope the depth of his feelings were the same.

And staying together in Ms. Blackburn's house only made him warmer, and fonder. It was easy to pretend, tucked away on the edge of the North Sea, that the rest of the world didn't exist. He was content to play house and share his bed, though he suspected his heart might break when reality came crashing in once more. But until then, so long as the creature remained out of sight, Loxley could pretend that it wasn't there at all, creeping silver through the shadows, waiting for its next chance to strike.

On their eighth day as guests, Loxley was subjected to a series of experiments in which Thorncress tried to force the enchantment from his body with sheer brute magic, the results of which left Loxley wrapped in a quilt, huddled in front of the fireplace and nursing a tea.

"I do not feel any different except that I am now very sore," he proclaimed, extending one hand from his blanket so that Thorncress could put the charm to it again. His finger burned and blackened as it always did, and they conceded defeat once more.

"Tomorrow we might try sweating it out of you, as with a sickness," Thorncress said, lacking enthusiasm as he sat down beside him. He glanced sideways at Loxley. "Are you ill? You've been wearing that scarf for days."

The burn on his neck had begun to peel in earnest, great flakes of dead, black skin coming away every time he touched it.

"I'm not used to that wind off the coast, is all. I feel fine, other than the bruises I'm sure I've incurred from your magic."

"It was worth a try."

Loxley was beginning to think otherwise. Despite all their combined knowledge of Faerie, scraped together from decades of work, neither Thorncress nor Ms. Blackburn could land on a single idea to break the enchantment, nor even lessen its hold on him.

"Perhaps Ms. Blackburn had the right idea all along, and I should build myself a house from the ground up, fortified with every charm and ward I can lay my hands on. If my curse can't be broken, then . . ."

"You'll spend the rest of your life in the same four walls?" Thorncress asked, doubtfully.

"It needn't be so bad. I could have my books, and perhaps—perhaps a companion, to make it more bearable." He had been content, once, to live as a monk with his books and his scholarly research, but he wasn't sure he could return to such an existence, having sampled Thorncress' constant companionship. Not that such a man would ever suffer to live trapped within a single house for the rest of his days.

"Grace isn't cursed," Thorncress pointed out. "Charms and wards will protect you for a while, but it's only a matter of time before the creature works out some way around or through them."

"I don't suppose we can stay here until that happens?"

"I think we may wear out our welcome before it does. Grace didn't expect to be hosting us a week when she opened her door."

Ms. Blackburn waved him off. "I'd not have invited you in if I didn't mean it."

"There's some difference between inviting an old friend in for the night, and having folks stay indefinitely," Thorncress countered.

"You've been most hospitable," Loxley added. "I didn't really mean—"

"I know you didn't," she said firmly. "You're welcome to stay, but Mr. Thorncress is right. Sooner or later, your fae is going to find a way inside, and it'll do you no good to be sitting here at ease when it happens."

❋ ❋ ❋

That night, as he lay in bed, Loxley imagined the creature conducting its own experiments outside, testing the strengths and limits of Ms. Blackburn's protections, and he clenched his fists in the sheets to keep from shaking. At his back, he sensed that Thorncress was likewise awake, perhaps even occupied with the same fretful supposition.

Yet, when Thorncress finally spoke, it was not on the matter Loxley had expected.

"These un-Christian thoughts you say you harbour. Will you tell me of them?"

Loxley's cheeks burned. He had thought the matter of his being a changeling was long dropped, but it seemed Thorncress had merely taken the time to mull it over, examining Loxley's fear from every angle.

"I would forgo your judgement, sir. I have enough of my own as it is."

"I've said before that you judge yourself too harshly."

Loxley felt rather than saw Thorncress turn onto his side to face him, and he forced himself to do the same.

"Do you wish to hurt people?" Thorncress asked.

"Certainly not! I could never."

"Or yourself?"

Loxley was sure that the lie was written plainly on his face. Were it daylight, Thorncress could read it in an instant. "No, nor myself."

"Then what could be so terrible that you would rather be found a changeling than take responsibility?"

"I have certain inclinations," Loxley said slowly. "They do no harm except, perhaps, to my social standing, but the fear is a terrible thing. If my wants are so unnatural, I thought—I hoped—that I, too, was unnatural. It could have excused me, you see."

He raised his eyes and found Thorncress' gaze dark and thoughtful. His eyes looked liquid in the dark; his eyelashes were long and sooty, casting delicate shadows on his cheek.

"I take your meaning." Thorncress' voice was a low rumble, the tone somehow reassuring, and when he didn't immediately move away, Loxley relaxed fractionally. "What is it that you want, Mr. Loxley?"

"Only love."

"That doesn't seem such an unnatural thing. Do you fear my judgement? Or do you fear the wrath of God?"

"I fear losing you," he confessed.

"Then that is easily settled. Such sins hurt no one, and I'll not turn you away for them."

"But you do consider it a sin. Being a Catholic, I suppose you must."

"It's a sin, but not one that bothers me. I turned from God's path so long ago, it would be hypocritical of me to judge such minor ones as that. Do you not consider it a sin?"

"I don't see how one can both preach love and condemn it in the same breath. I fear a public hanging far more than I fear Hell."

Thorncress rumbled an agreement.

"Though," Loxley added, "if I'm stolen to Faerie, I suppose Hell won't matter much anyway."

"True enough." Thorncress' gaze turned searching. "You keep many things from me, Mr. Loxley. I hope this conversation has given you some relief."

"Some. I do take comfort in knowing you'd not cast me aside for it." Tentatively, he spread one hand over Thorncress' chest, feeling the steady thrum of his heart through his shirt. They had no way of breaking the creature's enchantment, and his days were surely numbered. For once in his life, he wanted to be brave. "But knowing that I have such desires is not the same as knowing that I desire you."

Thorncress stilled for a second, and Loxley held his breath.

"No," Thorncress finally said. "I'd not turn you away for that, either."

Loxley leaned in, closing the scarce gap between them and pressing their lips together. Thorncress' lips were chapped from the cold, and the drag of his stubble against Loxley's skin was rough, but his mouth was warm and his touch was firm. He threaded his fingers through Loxley's curls, holding him close as their legs entangled and their bodies pulled together like magnets. Loxley couldn't help the moan that escaped him. In that moment, he didn't care that Ms. Blackburn was in the next room, and that she might overhear them. Between their shared heat and the heady feeling of Thorncress' mouth against his, Loxley's fear burned away and left nothing but pure want in its wake. Nothing about Thorncress' touch felt wrong.

They both drew back at the same time, breathing heavily as they sought to catch their breath. Thorncress' dark eyes looked black, his palm laying heavy over Loxley's collarbone.

"I like this look on you," he said, his voice low.

"What look is that?"

"Pleased. And overwhelmed. Are you still afraid?"

"In London, I felt like everyone was watching me. Here, it's as if I've moved beyond the reach of the law. If the rest of my life is to be governed by Faerie rule, why should I care about the laws of men?" Loxley's stomach lurched, despite his words. Such unnatural acts were scorned the country over. English law still applied in the north; he could hang in Scarborough as surely as in London. He curled his fingers around a strand of Thorncress' hair, privately marvelling that he was allowed to touch it. "Perhaps, if I've slipped from God's attention, so too have I slipped from the eyes of the law. As if I'm fading from the world entirely."

"Does that trouble you?"

Loxley took a deep breath. "It should. But here, like this? I could be persuaded that it's not so terrible a thing."

"Then let me persuade you some more."

Their mouths joined again, hot and insistent, and Loxley threw himself into the sensation of it. He wanted to map the planes and angles of Thorncress' body, to feel his sweat-slicked skin. It was wild and it was reckless, but Loxley had been careful all his life, and it had earned him nothing but years of loneliness, and a fae enchantment he couldn't break. He smiled against Thorncress' lips.

"What amuses you?" Thorncress asked, moving his attention from Loxley's mouth to his jaw, trailing biting kisses along the underside, above the scarf's thick ridge.

"I feel like I've wasted my life, up until this moment."

"And that gives you cause to smile?"

"Maybe. Maybe I'm damned. Maybe Faerie has had me since I was a boy, and God hasn't looked my way in years. I've wasted so much time worrying—"

Thorncress paused in his ministrations, propping himself up on his elbows in order to look Loxley in the eye.

"It might bother me later," Loxley said. "But not now."

With a smile, Thorncress leaned down and kissed him soundly. Pushing into the touch, Loxley worked his hands under Thorncress' shirt, untucking it from his trousers to seek out warm skin. He spread his palms over Thorncress' broad back, appreciating the way his muscles shifted under his hands, and the animal heat of his body. Tugging the scarf loose to kiss his throat, Thorncress positioned one knee in between Loxley's thighs before flattening down against him, and Loxley moaned appreciatively. But he wasn't so lost in the moment that he failed to direct Thorncress to the unburned side of his neck, tugging on his hair to move him into the new position. If Thorncress suspected anything, he didn't show it, but Loxley worked him to distraction just in case.

"Tell me what you want," Thorncress murmured, open-mouthed against his throat.

"Anything," Loxley gasped. "Anything you can give me."

"You won't regret it, come morning?"

"No. Not if it's with you."

Thorncress' touch was nothing like the creature's. He ran hot while it was as ice; his kisses burned like fire where its kisses felt like the biting teeth of frost. Where the creature only ever took without asking, its long, clever fingers pickpocketing Loxley's mind, Thorncress was generous. He bent himself to Loxley's needs, seemingly intent on drawing sounds from him, coaxing him to soft cries and stifled moans.

They undressed each other with clumsy hands, shedding their clothes without a care as to where they fell. There was a desperation to their touches: desperate to stay quiet and avoid Ms. Blackburn's attention; and desperate to draw what pleasure they could from their bodies before their circumstances caught up to them in the less forgiving light of day.

Loxley wouldn't have dared touch Thorncress in the daylight. In part because he was too used to hiding his desires, but also because in the light, the ragged burn on his neck would be immediately obvious. In the dark of their bedroom, under the covers, Loxley could still hide it, even without his scarf. If Thorncress touched him there, he would stop everything to investigate, and then Loxley's secret would be dragged out without him having to confess at all. It would be better if Thorncress chanced upon it in that way.

Still, Loxley couldn't help but hide the mark. His hands refused to guide Thorncress to it; his tongue turned leaden and foiled his every attempt to catch Thorncress' attention. Frustrated, he buried his hands in Thorncress' hair, which Thorncress took as encouragement to move his mouth lower on Loxley's body.

Loxley wanted to tell him about the creature's testimony, the bruise that marked him, its subsequent burning, the hawthorn apple—all of it, everything—but when he opened his mouth to let it come pouring forth, all he managed was a bitten-off cry.

At the sound, Thorncress paused and lifted his head. "What do you want me to do?"

Loxley stared at him, flushed, his hair in disarray, lips still parted. Thorncress gazed back at him from where he was settled between Loxley's thighs. He looked like he belonged there, his hair loose from its tie and hanging around his face in waves. His eyes burned dark in the shadows, inquisitive as he awaited Loxley's reply.

When Loxley realized that Thorncress wasn't going to move until he answered, he said in a hoarse voice, "Please."

"Please what?"

With a shaking hand, Loxley reached to touch his face, dragging one fingertip down his cheek to press against his lips—those lips that had, only seconds ago, been pressed to Loxley's skin. "Please, kiss me," he whispered. "Anywhere. Don't take your mouth off me."

Never looking away, Thorncress took Loxley's fingertip into his mouth, his tongue warm and wet against the sensitive pad. Loxley swallowed. He would let Thorncress do whatever he wanted, anything at all. Thorncress kissed his way up to Loxley's knuckles before turning into his palm, kissing next the delicate underside of his wrist, and the inner crook of his elbow. Loxley quivered from the attention. He had always told himself that he didn't need anyone. It was better to be lonely than in prison, after all. But so many nights he had lain awake and yearned for someone to touch him, to know what he wanted without having to be told.

Thorncress seemed to know his most intimate desires without Loxley having to say a word. He kissed his way up to Loxley's shoulder, mouthing along his collarbone before trailing down his abdomen, following the faint line of muscles that bisected his torso. His stubble scratched the sensitive skin there, and Loxley shivered and bit his lip, one hand tangled in Thorncress' hair— not directing, but merely holding on, as if he needed to be joined to the man in as many ways as possible, never to let go.

Finally, Thorncress returned to between his thighs, a comfortable weight draped across his hips. Loxley held his breath, his lower lip caught between his teeth. Looking down the length of his own body, he met Thorncress' gaze, shadowed by those long, dark lashes. "Do you still consider it a sin?"

Thorncress smiled sharply. "If the devil wants us, he must fight Faerie for the privilege."

Loxley pushed up to kiss him again, their mouths meeting in a hungry clash, fingers wound through hair and hands grasping at shoulders like they meant to melt into each other and become a single body without beginning or end. Thorncress rolled his hips against Loxley's in a steady, maddening rhythm, as constant as the sea, and Loxley wrapped his legs around Thorncress' thighs, urging him on. As their breaths came faster, they broke the kiss to pant raggedly into one another's throats, their skin slick with sweat, and their moans dark and wordless. They crested together, losing the rhythm as pleasure crashed over them in a wave, which they rode until they were both wrung-out and sated.

Thorncress collapsed on top of Loxley, his face buried in the crook of Loxley's neck, mouthing at the skin of his shoulder. Loxley lay under him, chest heaving as his breathing slowly steadied, one arm wrapped around Thorncress' shoulders to keep him in place. In a moment, they would cool, and their sweat would dry, but Loxley didn't want to move and break the heady glow of their intimacy. He wanted to kiss Thorncress again, to coax him into another round, but he would be content to fall asleep in his arms, as well.

It was sleep that won out. Loxley shut his eyes, pleasantly exhausted and secure. He was dimly aware of Thorncress rising from the bed to fetch a cloth to clean them, before returning to Loxley's side and throwing a heavy arm over his waist. Loxley drifted off in his embrace, his face tilted towards Thorncress as if searching for his kiss unconsciously, and for the first time, the creature didn't haunt his thoughts. He could still sense its presence beyond the house, but it could only lurk on the outskirts of his consciousness.

※ ※ ※

Loxley woke to weak morning light slanting over the pillows, and a shift in the mattress that indicated that Thorncress had sat up. Blinking, he furrowed his brow as he focused on Thorncress' shape. The man was sitting on the edge of the bed, dressed in his shirt and trousers, though his hair was still loose and wild around his face. Loxley offered him a smile as he rubbed the sleep from his eyes.

"Good morning," he said around a yawn, indulging in a full-body stretch. He hadn't slept so well in so long, unplagued by anxiety or nightmarish visitations. And Thorncress—he had tasted the man, and heard the sounds he made when—

Thorncress didn't reply. Frowning, Loxley sat up, but a hand on his forearm prevented him from moving further.

"What's wrong?"

Thorncress was staring at him. Not at his face, but in the vicinity of his collar, and— Oh.

Loxley froze, his throat working as he swallowed. He had forgotten, in his afterglow of pleasure, what he had meant to be hiding. Sitting naked before Thorncress' piercing gaze, he had no way to hide the ugly burn on his neck, nor any way to feign ignorance.

Moving slowly, as if Loxley were a wild animal at risk of lashing out, Thorncress raised one hand, ghosting over the area without touching it. Loxley flinched back, more from shame than fear, but Thorncress stopped abruptly all the same.

"Why did you hide this?"

"I didn't want you to know," Loxley said, voicelessly.

Thorncress was silent for a moment, examining the burn. Loxley didn't know how it looked in the morning light, but he could feel it. The skin was drawn tight, as if stretched, and felt dry and itchy. If he scratched it, he knew it would peel under his fingernails, the burned flesh coming away in long strips, like tearing old wallpaper from the plaster. He had done it before. Tucking his hands under his thighs, he looked away, unable to meet Thorncress' gaze.

"You did this to yourself?"

Wordlessly, he nodded.

Thorncress took Loxley's right wrist, drawing his hand up. As he had done before, he inspected the burn on his fingertip, where the skin was blackened over that sliver of a scar.

"You kept trying to burn Faerie out of you. It didn't work. What else don't you want me to know?"

Loxley's gaze flickered to his coat, where it hung on the bedpost. Flinching, he pulled his attention away, but it was too late: Thorncress' sharp eyes had already caught the movement. Releasing his wrist—Loxley bit his tongue and tried not to feel the sting of dismissal—Thorncress rose from the bed and went directly to the coat, picking it up by the collar as one might scruff an animal, and held it out.

"You cannot tell me?"

Mutely, Loxley shook his head, at once terrified and drowning in relief at the thought of Thorncress uncovering the last of his secrets. His frown deepening with every passing second, Thorncress turned the coat pockets out, beginning at the breast and working his way down. When at last he hit the pocket that hid the hawthorn apple, Loxley drew a breath so sharp that Thorncress glared at him, though his glare couldn't quite mask his concern.

He drew the haw out. There was no reason for Loxley's heart to clench so horribly at its reveal, but he couldn't help the shiver that coursed through him at the sight of someone else handling it. As if it were a precious gift meant for him alone.

"How long have you had this?"

Loxley forced his throat to cooperate. "I don't know. I only noticed it recently, but." He swallowed. "Perhaps all my life."

Thorncress closed his fingers around it, and Loxley felt that he had wrapped his fingers around his throat, so suddenly did the life feel choked from him.

"I think," said Thorncress in a low voice, "it's time to go back to your house. I wish to see that hawthorn tree you kept from me the first time around."

CHAPTER EIGHT

THE HAWTHORN TREE

"I'm sorry," Loxley said.

"The fault was mine," Thorncress replied shortly. "I knew that the nature of your enchantment kept you from telling me certain details. I should have uncovered them myself, with or without your cooperation. I became complacent."

Ms. Blackburn met them in the kitchen, her brows knitted as she acknowledged the freezing atmosphere. "You're leaving, I take it?"

"We should have left days ago." Thorncress wasn't looking at either of them. "His old house holds secrets that I mean to pry out."

"Eat something before you go. The house will still be there, whether you leave now or in an hour."

"We have food," Thorncress said flatly.

"So do I," Ms. Blackburn countered. "You're not a fool, John. You know better than to turn down an offered meal. Now, sit."

Loxley sat silently as Thorncress and Ms. Blackburn put together a modest breakfast. He wanted to help, if only to keep occupied, but Thorncress had glared him down. He stared at his hands, folded on the tabletop. THE APPLE was still faintly visible against the wood, like a ghost, invisible but to those who knew where to look.

"You found out what's tied his tongue," Ms. Blackburn said. It wasn't a question.

Loxley forced a brittle smile, not raising his eyes. "I've no secrets left to me."

She brought over two cups of black tea while Thorncress carried plates of eggs and toast, slathered thick with preserves. "It might hurt now, Mr. Loxley, but it's best to cut those secrets out sooner than later, before they fester." She nodded to his plate. "Eat up. I've something else to give you, before you go."

She went to the door and Thorncress stalked after her, ignoring his food. Loxley watched them pull the door shut behind them, standing at the corner of the house under the rowan tree. Ms. Blackburn was occupied with the tree itself while Thorncress spoke, gesturing between them with a terrible scowl. Heaving a sigh, Loxley turned to his food. The egg was glossy yellow and white, running thick yolk into the toast's crust, where drops of wildberry jam smeared against the dish. It smelled delicious, but though his stomach growled, he had little appetite. He should be ravenous, after the exertions of the previous night, but he could only pick at his plate, forcing down one bite after the other.

Ms. Blackburn returned a moment later, with Thorncress in tow.

"Give me your coat, Mr. Loxley, and I'll sew another charm onto it." She held out one hand expectantly.

His coat was folded over the back of his chair, and he obediently passed it to her, nibbling at his toast as she settled in at the table with a sewing box and two twigs clipped from the rowan's branch.

"For protection," she explained, "since nothing else has worked."

The twigs were arranged in the shape of the cross, and she fixed them in place with a length of red ribbon, winding it deftly around them until they couldn't shift against one another, and then stitching the cross to the front of his coat, over the breast, with a few quick passes of the needle.

"You keep this on you, and you wear the iron charm I gave you at the start. It's not enough to break your enchantment, but it should keep your creature from getting its teeth in you again."

She handed him a short length of cord, which he threaded through the iron charm to tie around his neck, so it rested against his chest beneath his shirt. The metal was freezing, but it didn't burn him there.

"Thank you, Ms. Blackburn. You're most generous."

"It's nothing. Finish your toast. And you, Mr. Thorncress," she added. "I can hear you lurking about, ignoring your breakfast. Scowling and going hungry won't solve anything."

Thorncress took his seat and set into his food, though his heavy glare remained. Loxley avoided his eye as best he could, but in a kitchen so small, their silence turned the air frigid, and he itched to ride out again, if only so the wind and the sound of the horses would give them some excuse to keep silent.

When they finished eating, Thorncress cleared the dishes as Ms. Blackburn went to the cupboards, retrieving a small jar that she gave to Loxley. The salve inside was thick and shiny, and smelled sharp.

"For burns," she said, her sightless eyes staring into him. "Applied once in the morning and once at night, to stave off infection."

"Thank you," he said quietly, slipping it into his pocket as he donned his coat.

Across the room, Thorncress set the last of the dishes aside to dry and followed suit, coming to stand beside him. "We'd best be off. Thank you for breakfast, Grace. And everything else."

"Take care, the both of you. And John?"

Thorncress paused, one hand on the door. His hair hung in his face, obscuring his features, but his tone was heavy. "I know."

❈ ❈ ❈

The ride back to Pickering was a miserable one. Sleet rained down cold and wet, plastering itself to their hats and sticking in the horses' manes, but Thorncress marched them grimly on. Loxley grew colder and stiffer the longer they rode, and guilt and panic coiled within him, gnawing at one another like wild dogs. The guilt wanted him to grovel and make amends for his deception, unwilling as it had been, but the panic urged him to turn his horse and ride as hard and as fast as he could away from Thorncress—away from his glower, his heavy disappointment, and his steadfast insistence on returning to that damned hawthorn tree.

But he had pocketed the haw after its discovery, and Loxley felt it like a tug on his soul. He could no more ride away than he could leave behind his own heart. How did such a little thing have such a hold on him? When Thorncress touched it, Loxley squirmed. It felt as if he were being touched in some secret place where no one had the right to lay their hands, somewhere deep and private. His insides twisted at the sensation and his mind shied away. He had to keep himself from lurching forward and snatching the haw back, returning it to his own safekeeping. If Thorncress were to destroy it, crushing it under the heel of his boot, would Loxley's life be crushed out with it? It was an awful fear that churned inside him, turning his stomach to acid.

But, because he couldn't explain such an irrational reaction, he kept his hands clasped stiffly around the reins, and he followed at Thorncress' heels, biting his tongue against the pleas that would have tumbled, desperate, from his lips.

The sleet changed to snow as they rode through Pickering at twilight. As the sky darkened from blue-grey to charcoal, fat flakes whispered down from the clouds, catching in Loxley's eyelashes and melting against his cheeks. He blinked them away, the wetness feeling like tears.

Thorncress halted outside the house, dismounting in a sweep of his cloak to push the creaky gate open and lead his horse into the yard. Loxley sat frozen in his saddle, his shoulders hunched and fingers numb around the reins. Thorncress spared him a glance.

"Are you coming?"

"Please." Loxley couldn't feel his lips; the word came out bloated and misshapen. "Please, don't do this. Don't go in."

"You know we must."

Without another word, Thorncress turned his back to Loxley and entered the yard, guiding his horse unerringly around the side to the back, and Loxley was helpless but to follow him.

It looked eerier in the low light. The snow clung to the rooftop and the trees' naked branches, turning everything ghostly and alien. Loxley remembered the trees best in late summer: their broad, dark trunks and rich green leaves dappling the yard in gentle shadows, the haw apples nestled amid the long grass like tiny treasures to be collected. The bare trees in winter, he saw only from his window. They creaked and groaned, the wind rattling his name as if on a dying breath, the frost sprites drawing faces on his window, and watching him pale-eyed from the fireplace.

He hadn't thought of such things in years.

Standing side by side in the yard, facing the silent army of black, barren trees, Thorncress reached into his pocket and retrieved Loxley's haw, offering it to him. Numbly, Loxley held out his hand to accept it, and Thorncress tipped it into his palm. It sat there, whole and unharmed and as plain as any other haw Loxley had ever seen, but the relief at having it returned was overwhelming. His fingers curled around it of their own volition, and though he was ashamed of the enormity of his relief, he couldn't mask it. Thorncress watched him in silence before nodding to the line of trees at the back of the property, where the hawthorn stood among them like a king.

"Don't talk. Don't think. Just go."

With a shuddering breath, Loxley steeled his body and emptied his mind. He moved like a sleepwalker, his steps careful as he headed for the trees. He couldn't think about Thorncress, or the charm around his neck or the haw in his hand. He focused solely on the hawthorn tree, and the companionship it had offered him as a child. The companion . . .

He stumbled, his trousers caught by a thatch of nettles, and fell to his knees. His hands pressed against the hard, snow-dusted ground, cold even through his gloves, and his breath gusted out in a plume of frost. Before him rose the hawthorn's trunk, the oldest tree in the yard, standing between the house and the very edge of the forest. Its bark looked black in the dwindling dusk, grooves etched deep into the wood, gnarled and ancient. He had played in its shade every summer for years, collecting the haws that dropped, laughing and telling stories to his—

Talking to his—

With a trembling hand, Loxley reached out and brushed the weeds aside. There, nestled close to the ground, covered by the husks of dead plants and soon to be hidden under the coming snow, a tiny mark was etched into the wood. Loxley stared at it until tears stung his eyes, startling in their heat. No more than four strokes to make the marking. If he looked at it from the corner of his eye—a fleeting glimpse, a passing fancy—it looked almost like a man, his arms flung out in dance.

"I remember you," Loxley whispered, his heart in his throat, tight with dread.

❃ ❃ ❃

Loxley didn't have a name or a face for the little figure that lived in the hawthorn tree, but he called it his friend. He recognized it in the birds that chattered from the treetops, and the insects that buzzed in the leaves, and the red shine of the hawthorn apples where they lay in the grass. The bark never scabbed over and the mark never faded, no matter how many seasons passed, and he never questioned the presence he felt—as if there were someone in the yard with him, playing at his side. An imaginary friend, a companion fit for a lonely little boy.

But sometimes the presence grew hungry and the mood turned impatient, as if there were someone watching him from just beyond the forest's border, and sometimes he heard his name called in a thin, reedy voice that carried on the breeze when the birds fell silent, and it didn't feel companionable at all.

He hurried inside on those days, when the eyes on the back of his neck sent shivers down his spine, and the sound of his name made his hairs stand on end. He could never place the source of his discomfort, and so he never mentioned it. There was no one lurking in the trees; there was no one whispering his name. But he felt safer tucked away inside, all the same.

That hungry presence never haunted him two days in a row. When he next emerged into the yard, skipping back to his favourite tree to check on the little dancing man, the birds called and the insects hummed and the breeze rustled through the leaves as if nothing was amiss, and Loxley returned to his usual games with his invisible friend.

He collected haws. As the summer grew long and lazy, slowly turning its attention to the coming autumn, he plucked them from the branches to pocket, bringing home handfuls every evening for his mother to make into preserves. There was something comforting in the feel of them: the way he could stroke his thumb over the skin and it would glow warmly from his body heat, firm and smooth and just the right size to tuck against his palm. He spent hours picking them, some days, basking in the sun and talking to his tree-bark friend. The hawthorn, its canopy spread like a crown against the sky, dappled the yard in blue-green shadows as the sun shone gold above. During those summer days, Loxley was fearless and content.

But as the days grew shorter and the shadows stretched long at twilight, the atmosphere shifted with the sun. He felt those eyes boring into his back more often, and his name hissed from between the branches. He spent shorter hours in the yard, and the frost nipped at his heels as he ran back to the house, rolling the haws between his palms in pagan prayer. As the sun set, the trees reached out their spindly fingers and the nettles caught at his trouser legs, clinging to him and trying to draw him back to the yard. The chill breeze ruffled his hair and carried on it a keening whisper whose words he could never understand, but which sent a curl of unease through his stomach, and anxiety bolting through his brain. Pulling his coat tight, he clenched his fingers around the haws and forged on, back to the safety of his house.

Inside, when it grew colder still and autumn slunk away before winter's reach, with the fire crackling brightly in the hearth, and in his parent's company, it was easy to forget the woods and the trees. But at night, when the fire burned low and the lamps were dimmed, the frost drew patterns across the glass of his bedroom window. They looked like strange, misshapen faces with sharp teeth and long, reaching fingers. Loxley hid beneath the covers on those nights, when the frost reached too high. In the mornings, the patterns melted away before the dawn, but the wind still whistled strangely, and the trees looked foreign and threatening without their leaves.

In the spring of his twelfth year, his parents took him away from little Pickering. Loxley had never been to London, but they told him that he would go to a better school there, and meet more boys his own age. The excitement of a new place—a whole entire city, practically another world—ran roughshod over any sense of loss. The only thing to which he needed to bid goodbye was the hawthorn.

Crouching down amid the nettles and the wildflowers, heedless of the soil that stained his knees, he sought out the little figure in the bark, his one constant companion.

"I won't be seeing you anymore," he said solemnly. "I'm going away to London, where there won't be any trees for you to live in. But I'm keeping this." He had saved one haw apple from the previous season, carefully drying it by the fire. It should have withered and wizened, but instead it was perfectly preserved, like a specimen in amber, its skin dark and warm and smooth. Overhead, the delicate, newborn leaves shivered in the breeze. "So that I won't forget about you. I hope you won't forget me, either. One day, when I'm grown, I'll come back."

It was a child's promise, with little thought put into it. In truth, he wouldn't miss the yard's ever-changing moods, the whispers and the sense of some unseen threat he had never been able to shake, no matter how old he grew.

Before he rose, he pressed one finger to the figure, in a gentle farewell. But the rough bark caught his skin and a single drop of blood welled up and fell onto the tree trunk. The droplet seeped into the bark, disappearing into the pale, scratched form of the dancing figure. Frowning, Loxley stuck his finger in his mouth before returning his hand to the haw, pocketing it, and dashing back to the house, where his parents were readying to leave.

The cut itself was insignificant: a tiny dash across the pad of his right index finger, easily cleaned and quickly healed. But it left a thin white scar that persisted through the years, even after Loxley forgot all about his yearly ritual with the haw apples, and how the woods changed with the seasons, and how the frost seemed to watch him, painting sharp and wicked faces against his windowpane.

In his pocket, that solitary haw rested, its skin stained with a single drop of blood.

❖ ❖ ❖

Loxley sat on the ground as the snow piled up on his shoulders and his hat, gently burying him under a cold, white blanket. "What can I do?"

For a moment, Thorncress didn't answer. Loxley felt him as a solid presence at his back, standing tall and dark as the night crept on. "This creature knows your name and has your blood," he finally said. "Both freely given, if unwitting." His words sounded like a death knell. "Small wonder we couldn't break it. There's nothing more to be done, short of killing the thing."

Loxley pulled in a ragged breath. "Can it be done?"

"As easily as killing anything else." Thorncress' hand fell on Loxley's shoulder, a tired, heavy weight. "Come, Mr. Loxley. You'll catch your death sitting here."

Loxley didn't know if that would be such a bad thing, but he struggled to his feet and followed Thorncress back to his old house. It was as they had left it, with one bed pulled out to sit in front of the empty hearth. Loxley sat on the edge of the mattress as Thorncress hauled an armful of wood inside and set about lighting a fire, coaxing the kindling to take the flame until it was crackling and spitting, smoke curling up the chimney. When the fire was burning steadily and needed no more gentling, Thorncress came to sit beside him.

"Tell me about your neck."

The burn was raw, the blisters having been rubbed open again by Loxley's scarf. "The creature comes nightly to mark me. Laying claim, or strengthening its hold on me, I don't know. There was some respite at Ms. Blackburn's, but I fear it will return now that we're gone." He folded his fingers together in his lap, staring at them. "Do you blame me for all of this?"

"No. I understand the strength of faerie magic. It's not your fault."

"I gave myself to it." Loxley's voice broke and he dug his nails into the skin of his opposite hand to ground himself. Now that the secret of the hawthorn tree had been pulled out, the floodgates had opened, and he could hardly stop himself from spilling more.

"You were a child," Thorncress said fiercely. "You didn't know."

Loxley tried to offer him a weak smile. "I've been a fool all my life, it seems."

Thorncress shook his head, his hair falling loose from its tie as he put one arm around Loxley's shoulders. Surprised by the touch, it took Loxley a second to lean into it, burrowing into the warmth of his embrace.

"Wisdom cannot save you," Thorncress said. "Faerie will take as it pleases."

Loxley listened to the steady beating of Thorncress' heart. "Who did it take from you?"

Thorncress' heart skipped a beat and Loxley bit his lip, waiting. When Thorncress finally spoke, his voice was rough and ruined. "My sister." He stood, disengaging from Loxley entirely, and paced to the window. "You should rest, Mr. Loxley. The charms will safeguard you from the worst of the creature's efforts, even here."

"You're not joining me?"

"Later." Thorncress glanced back at him. His features were drawn, and exhaustion and old grief weighed heavily on his brow, but he didn't look angry anymore. "Go to sleep. I'll be here."

Hesitantly, Loxley nodded and shed his outer layers, crawling under the blankets to curl up on the cold mattress alone. When he looked over, Thorncress had turned back to the window, resting his forehead against the glass. He held a piece of paper between his fingers, its edges worn to softness, and though he turned it over between his hands, he didn't read it.

※ ※ ※

Loxley dreamed he was standing in his childhood bedroom. The room had no roof; above him, the sky was vast and full of tiny, glittering stars, like pinpricks torn through black velvet. Tipping his head back, he watched his breath curl out in a plume of frost, shimmering up to the stars as if it meant to join them and build its own galaxy.

When he lowered his gaze, the creature was watching him from the other side of the window.

It stood upright like a man, but with hunched shoulders, its arms hanging at odd angles, like an animal mimicking human stance. It stared at him with wide, pale eyes, too alien for the expression to be called resentment. Perhaps hunger was a better word for it. Loxley would call it yearning, if that weren't such a human emotion, and the creature was far from human. Yet when he looked at it, no more than a thin sheet of glass separating them, he felt not fear, but a dreadful kind of loneliness that caused his bones his ache and his heart to throb like it was being strangled in his chest.

He wanted to open the window, to reach out his arms and offer himself to the creature, to let it take him in whatever way it wished, if only that would stop the terrible longing that emanated from its eyes.

He wanted to draw the curtains and crawl back into bed, under the covers, and hide there like a child, whispering prayers to a deaf God as if that could protect him.

"You never came back," the creature said. "You promised. Waited, I."

"I'm sorry. I couldn't remember. I didn't think you were real."

The creature bared its teeth, looking hurt or angry, Loxley couldn't tell. "Doesn't matter. Found you. Brought you back."

"I don't want to be here."

It shook its head, a short, sharp motion, bird-like. "Promised," it insisted, and then drew closer. Loxley took a step back, but the creature didn't open the window. It merely pressed one long-fingered hand to the glass, its head tilted inquisitively. "Why do you keep yourself away? Charms and curses. Promised mine, from your golden youth till the end of time. Trying to cut me out, sweet prince? Burn me away?" It smiled. Its teeth were very long, and very sharp, gleaming like moonstones. "Cannot escape the promise made. Open the window, little woodland prince. Autumn child. Open the window, open the door."

Loxley had one hand wrapped around the charm at his throat, the other curled around his bloodied haw. Above, the stars wheeled and screamed in the sky. He drew a deep breath—frost ached in his lungs—

And he woke to the sound of howling.

CHAPTER NINE

ROSA'S TALE

He couldn't place the sound, at first. It echoed through the house like there were no walls separating them from the wild. The cry started low, almost a moan, before soaring up in pitch, drifting on the wind. Thorncress was still at the window, rooted to the spot, staring out into the darkness. Rousing himself and pushing up to his elbows, Loxley called his name, but he didn't move. Unnerved, Loxley wondered for an instant if he was still trapped in that dream.

But Thorncress finally stirred, as if breaking from a trance.

"Her name was Rosa."

He turned, offering Loxley a glimpse of his profile. His hair hung in his face, and dark circles ringed his eyes, which had a faraway stare to them.

"She was sixteen; I was barely twenty. We were raised on all the old stories, but it didn't help." He drew a deep breath. He hadn't looked at Loxley once since he had started talking, and Loxley didn't dare interrupt. "She saw the hounds one morning. I wasn't there. She sent me a letter, though she knew I would never make it home in time. It reached me two days after her death."

"I'm sorry," Loxley said, knowing it was insufficient.

"She didn't tell anyone else. She didn't want to worry them, not when there was nothing to be done. I still carry her letter . . ." Trailing off, he stared into the shadows for a moment before continuing. "She described the hounds as great white beasts with eyes like foxfire, terrifying and beautiful. Like witnessing a natural disaster, something beyond comprehension. She said that even if she hadn't known the stories, she still would have understood that she was going to die." He paused for a moment. "Ma disappeared, after that. Returned to Scotland to find her people, though I don't know if they took her back. Da died not long after, sick from a broken heart. And I . . ."

Loxley swallowed. His knuckles were white in the sheets. "I heard you talking to Ms. Blackburn that night. Are you still trying to find her, your Rosa, after all this time?"

"Yes," Thorncress said simply.

"If she died . . ."

"Twenty-two years ago. But her soul passed into Faerie, not Heaven, and time passes differently there. I could still find her."

"Following her into Faerie is a death sentence."

Thorncress said nothing.

"Do you want to die?" Loxley finally asked in a broken voice.

"I made a promise." Thorncress' pitch was so low that Loxley strained to hear him. "I'm not one to break an oath."

"A promise to do what, exactly? Exact revenge?" Loxley's voice cracked in frightened desperation. "You cannot best a faerie hound—you'll only get yourself killed!"

"I've hunted the hounds all my life in the hopes that if I followed in her footsteps, I could find her again, wherever she is, and bring her back. And if not that, then at least I could join her, so she wouldn't be alone anymore."

"Surely she's released you from your promise by now."

"I've not released myself. She was my little sister; I should have been there. If nothing else, we could have gone together. She shouldn't have had to die alone."

Loxley could make no response to that. If he were to die at the creature's hands, he would appreciate whatever companionship Thorncress could offer, right up until the end. A hand to hold, a friend to sit by his side; someone to keep him from being quite so afraid as the dark and the cold crept in.

Shivering, he cast aside such morbid thoughts. What worked for men like Thorncress did no favours for those of Loxley's disposition. He could not imagine harbouring a death wish for so long. But then, perhaps he only lacked the proper motivation. He had no family to protect, no love for whom to die.

Then again, there were times when, under the enchantment, the danger felt more like a comfort, and being so near the thinning of the worlds felt almost like coming home. In those times, he found himself in deep rumination in the darkest hours of the night. Perhaps, if he studied that strange comfort a little harder, he might come to understand Thorncress' resolution.

"Very well," he said, though his heart broke at the words. "You must do as you feel is right. If you are duty-bound to your sister, then I am in no place to question you."

Thorncress inclined his head.

"But, at the risk of sounding selfish, I hope you do not fulfill your promise to her if it means leaving me alone. Don't go yet. I wouldn't know what to do."

Thorncress' gaze snapped up, and for a second he was as wide-eyed as if he had seen a ghost. Loxley had never seen him frightened, and the expression flashed by so quickly that he might have imagined it.

"I consider myself sworn to your cause as well. I never intended to leave before your creature was dealt with."

"By killing it."

"I don't know how else to break such an enchantment. You're blood-bound to it."

Slipping out from under the blankets, Loxley padded to the open hearth, where he stood by Thorncress' side. Though the fire was warm, Loxley still shook: from anxiety, from pent-up nerves, from grief at what was yet to come. Thorncress didn't move. He seemed shuttered, like he had closed himself off to Loxley, as impenetrable as Loxley had first imagined him. He had since learned that Thorncress was not made of stone—that he was in fact gentle, and caring, and as sensitive to grief and loss as any other man—but it was an illusion he wore, just as he wore his heavy coat, to shield him from the world. That he had brought it up again between them was troubling, for Loxley did not ever wish to be something from which Thorncress felt he needed shielding.

Cautiously, Loxley withdrew his haw apple from his coat on the chair. Thorncress allowed it, watching him with reserved curiosity. Neither of them spoke. Loxley clenched his fist until his knuckles hurt, the skin stretched tight over the bone and bleached white. Steeling himself and refusing to think too long on the action, he flung his hand out, casting the haw into the fire. Thorncress startled, twitching forward instinctively as if he meant to catch it, but Loxley held him back. Outside, something screamed: a cold, wailing keen, so intense and full of loss and fury that Loxley flinched back, hard.

"It has to burn. You mustn't let me take it back. I want to, I need to, but please, you have to stop me."

The haw's skin split open from the heat, the fruit inside hissing and spitting as if it had been picked that day, still fresh and sweet with juice. Charring, the skin peeled back and turned black as it burned, and Loxley swallowed a cry.

Joining their hands, Thorncress turned so they stood face to face. "Look at me. Don't look at the fire."

Loxley forced his eyes to Thorncress' face. His breathing was ragged, sweat breaking out across his brow as he fought the urge to plunge both hands into the hearth and dig the haw back out. It was his—it was a gift—it needed his protection, and he had thrown it aside—

"I made a mistake," he gasped, wrenching out of Thorncress' grasp. "I can't—"

"You will," Thorncress said firmly, catching him again and pulling him to his chest.

"I promised— I broke my promise—"

"You were a child enchanted. You didn't know the nature of your promise, and you shouldn't be held accountable."

Loxley choked on a sob, burying his face in Thorncress' shirt. "It's never going to let me go, is it?"

Thorncress hesitated. The fire cracked and popped, reducing the fruit to charcoal. "You should sleep, Mr. Loxley."

"Join me?"

He nodded and tugged Loxley back to the bed, ushering him under the covers before following suit. As soon as Thorncress was laying down, Loxley wrapped himself around him, tangling their limbs and laying his head on Thorncress' chest again, concentrating on the rise and fall of his breaths and the steady beating of his heart.

"Tomorrow," he whispered, curling his fingers in Thorncress' collar, "we'll go back to the trees. I'll burn away that mark on the trunk just as I tried to burn the ones on my skin."

Thorncress shifted and drew a breath as if he meant to speak, but Loxley hushed him.

"It was foolish; I know. I won't hurt myself again."

Thorncress pressed a kiss to Loxley's curls and held him tighter, but didn't say a word. Outside, that keening cry turned to growling and the sounds of something pacing the house's perimeter, but the creature didn't breach the walls. Eventually, lulled by their shared body heat and the gentle rhythm of his heart, Loxley fell asleep in Thorncress' arms, and whatever he dreamed, he couldn't remember on waking.

※ ※ ※

They stayed abed late into the morning, having been kept awake through much of the night by the creature's screams. Loxley was tempted to burrow deeper under the covers, to wrap his arms around Thorncress' shoulders and stay there, but Thorncress seemed disinclined to linger. He offered Loxley a fleeting kiss before rising and slipping into his boots, still wearing that mask from the previous night that made Loxley feel as if their relationship had backtracked a week in a single evening.

Outside, the snow covered the ground in a solemn blanket, and though it sparkled like diamonds in the pale sun, it looked as stark as the landscape ever did, and the glitter added no beauty to the place. The snow clung to the tree branches, too, coating them in ice, and to the sides of the trunks where the wind had blown. Loxley led the way through the back yard to his hawthorn tree, leaving a trail through the snow as he walked. He was strangely reluctant to destroy the smooth, even surface of the snow, though it was only an inch deep. It felt like an unnecessary intrusion; everything about the yard he had once played in now told him to turn back.

Kneeling by the hawthorn's trunk, he tugged the charm loose from under his shirt, lifting it over his head to hold between one gloved finger and a thumb. It couldn't hurt him through the leather, but he wished it would, just so he could feel something other than the cold coil of dread that waited in his stomach like a serpent. Thorncress stood at his shoulder, as silent and stark as the land.

Pressing the charm to the tree trunk wasn't as difficult as throwing the haw into the fire, but still, it hurt. Loxley felt the pain in his chest, like he was burning out his own heart by burning away the figure in the bark, and he gasped at the sudden pressure, lurching forward to brace himself with his other hand in the snow. Thorncress caught him by the shoulder, his fingers digging in painfully hard.

"Don't stop," he growled in a low whisper, "and don't look up."

Loxley felt the creature's presence before he saw it. The creature had never approached him in the light of day before—not since his boyhood, at least—and it was like seeing a dream made flesh. Its skin looked grey next to the pure white of the snow: grey like the clouds that had begun to send down a drift of flurries again, glittering in the air as they fell. It walked hunched over on all fours, snarling and spitting curses as it approached, though it halted just out of Thorncress' reach. Loxley ground his teeth and kept the charm pressed to the wood, even as the bark began to smoke and crackle.

"What are you doing?" the creature hissed, its back arched, cat-like. Its vertebrae stuck out like the keys of an instrument, stretching its too-thin skin tight. Paper-thin, blue veins showing through. It looked miserably cold in the snow. "Trying to burn me away?"

"Leave me alone," Loxley forced out, though his threat rang hollow. He didn't dare move from his spot at the base of the tree, depending on Thorncress to shield him.

"Can't," the creature swore. "Won't. You must come with me. Burn away the mark, burn away my gifts, your promises, but cannot burn the bond. You are mine. And yours, I."

"If you're mine, then I order you to go!" Loxley said, desperately. "Get out of here and leave me be!"

It prowled in a wide arc around them, tracing a semi-circle in the snow like a wild animal pacing its cage. "Cannot. Desperate, I. In need of you, your body, your soul."

"You can't have him." From his pocket, Thorncress drew a switchblade, a wicked-looking thing with a dull point and a handle worn smooth by years of use. Loxley's stomach flipped at the sight, in sudden fear of the prospect of spilled blood, but the creature only sneered.

"You save him? Know you, I. John Thorncress. Know your name, your deeds, wandering the north. Much to mourn, you think, but she is warm and shining in the sun. No more grey skies, no more freezing frost and driving snow. So far away, under the ground, behind the sky." It laughed in a sound like cracking ice. "Cannot touch her, Thorncress John. Cannot see her. In a better place than this, you know."

Thorncress stepped toward the creature, his arm held out straight at his side and at the end of it, the knife. The creature didn't back away. Instead, it rose to match him, lurching onto its hind legs so they were of a height, and curling its long fingers like talons.

"Kill me?' it spat. Its eyes burned like white fire, pale and furious. "You? You cannot kill me. Cannot even kill yourself!"

Thorncress lunged, arm and knife extended, and the creature twisted to avoid the blade before closing the distance between them in a flash, and leaping onto Thorncress' back, clinging to his shoulders and snapping at the exposed skin of his throat. Loxley shouted, caught between the need to intervene and the need to keep the charm against the tree, though he had nothing to offer in an altercation. Thorncress bucked, throwing his weight to the side as he bowled the creature to the ground and pinned it there. It writhed beneath him, teeth bared and eyes flashing, like a fox caught in the hunter's trap.

Thorncress pressed his knife to the creature's throat, and it stilled, wide-eyed.

"Tell me, since you cannot lie," Thorncress growled. "Is there any way short of killing you to make you leave him alone?"

"Only for him to give me what I want."

They were both still for a moment, and Loxley watched them, his heart in his throat. Thorncress would surely kill the creature; he had said enough times that such must be its fate. But he couldn't bear to see it happen. No mortal man had ever killed one of the Fair Folk before, not to his knowledge, and even if it was just some forgotten changeling child, it seemed an insult to the natural order of things.

Thorncress drew a ragged breath, his shoulders heaving, and Loxley flinched, quickly looking away. His grasp on the charm slipped for a split second, and in that instant, the creature moved like quicksilver. Thorncress pulled back; a line of ruby red droplets stained the snow beside him, and by it, his switchblade lay buried to the hilt. Clutching his hand where the creature had bit it, he reared back, but the creature was already on him, its fingers wrapped around his collar as it snarled and went for his throat once more.

Swearing, Loxley fumbled and dropped the charm, staggering to his feet—with the intent to retrieve the knife, or the charm, or simply to crash into the two of them and tear the creature away with his bare hands, he didn't know—when the creature stilled, and pulled back to look Thorncress in the eye. It wore a thoughtful expression that looked unsettlingly human on its alien face.

"Already claimed?"

Thorncress stiffened and reached for the knife, but the creature simply batted his hand aside, deceptively strong for something so slender and sickly-seeming. Its mouth stretched in a wide smile and it snapped its teeth in Thorncress' face, with a sharp bark like a dog. When he flinched back, it laughed and climbed off him, slinking back across the yard.

"Can wait, I. Can wait for the little autumn boy."

Thorncress snatched up the knife and flung it, but the creature darted out of reach, fleeing into the dark woods. The knife sank harmlessly into the snow, and Thorncress knelt there, staring after it. He made no move to rise or to reclaim the knife until Loxley went to him, placing one tentative hand on his shoulder.

"Thorncress? Did it hurt you?"

He shook his head.

"The blood," Loxley pressed, reaching for his hand.

Thorncress allowed him to take it. The thick leather of his glove had protected him from the worst of the creature's bite, but above the cuff, a ragged cut in the shape of an animal's teeth ran along his wrist and up his forearm. It seemed shallow, the bleeding already slowing to a crawl, but Loxley's heart hurt at the sight all the same.

"You should wash that."

Thorncress made a sound in his throat and rose stiffly to his feet, though he didn't draw his hand from Loxley's grasp. "It's alright."

"Then I will see it washed, if you're indifferent." At Thorncress' heavy look, Loxley sighed. "You've cared for me often enough. Let me do this."

Inside, as Loxley cleaned the bite with soap and water, Thorncress still and patient under his ministrations—or perhaps more vacant than patient—Loxley asked, "What did it mean by claimed?"

Thorncress watched the water run red for a moment, and Loxley watched him in the varnished mirror.

"Fae-touched," Thorncress finally said, not meeting his gaze. "As we talked about at Grace's. Not claimed, only marked."

Loxley remembered the way the charm had turned Thorncress' skin red and angry-looking without actually burning it. "I'll find a bandage to wrap this up."

"Don't bother. It'll heal just fine without."

CHAPTER TEN

THE HOUNDS

That night, they slept entwined again. They kissed for hours first, with Loxley stretched on top of Thorncress, covering him like a blanket and taking his face in his hands to kiss his lips, his jaw, his eyelids, the heat building between them until they were both sweating, the firelight dancing on their skins.

"We should have done this from the very beginning," Loxley murmured.

"A week ago, you were afraid to touch me."

"Would you have lain with me then?" Loxley asked curiously. "So soon after our meeting?"

"Perhaps not," Thorncress said, after a moment's consideration. "But if I could go back and do it again—yes."

"I didn't think you were often given to regrets."

"I'm not."

"Then don't dwell on it. We have time yet."

Thorncress curled both hands through Loxley's hair to bring him down to a fervent kiss.

"Or we could make the most of our time now," Loxley agreed, laughing breathlessly against Thorncress' lips. Thorncress merely shut his eyes and held him tighter, burying his face in Loxley's shoulder.

In the morning, Thorncress suggested that they cut down the hawthorn, though he looked ill at the thought. Loxley blanched at the idea.

"I know not what else to try. To destroy a hawthorn may be to invite a curse onto your head, but I can think of no worse fate than what awaits you already. You may destroy the talisman and the marks of the enchantment, cut and burn yourself to pieces, but the creature will keep growing stronger until even your charms cannot hold it at bay. And I cannot protect you forever."

Loxley stared out the window at the tree. It looked like it belonged in Faerie more than England: beautiful and sinister, standing tall and black against the storm clouds, its branches ringed in ice like jewelry.

"It won't work, will it?"

Thorncress hesitated, then sighed. "Not likely."

"Then let it stand. It seems a shame to kill it without good cause."

The snow had continued to fall all through the previous day and overnight, and it swirled in gusts and eddies outside the window, whistling around the door.

"Should we ride on?" Loxley asked, though he couldn't muster any enthusiasm for it. The horses were stabled in town; like him, he imagined they would prefer the comfort of a warm bed and a hot meal to the open road.

"Where would you go?"

Loxley had no ideas left. He couldn't go back to London; it felt a whole world away, and the creature had proven easily enough that it could find him there. Were they to wander the moors till spring? Thorncress may be at home in such stark lands, but they were still foreign to Loxley, harsh and unforgiving. He did not wish to spend his winter there.

"I don't know," he finally said. "I have nowhere left to turn."

"Then we'll stay here."

Loxley glanced at him, taken aback. Thorncress had always seemed so relentlessly driven, moving from one place to the next.

"At least for one more night," Thorncress said, with a tired shrug. "We've a bed and a fire here, and the snow will get worse before it lets up. It's no good setting off in a storm."

"Alright. It's as good a place as any, I suppose."

"Not quite." Thorncress' mouth twisted wryly as they both glanced at the hawthorn, its branches twisting in the wind.

"Well, it's hardly London, but it will do. I spent twelve years of my life here; what are a few more nights?"

They watched the snow for a few minutes in contemplation. It was beautiful, if Loxley imagined he were watching it from a London house, perhaps in the holiday season. With the fire crackling in the hearth and Thorncress at his side, he could pretend that they were comfortably ensconced and merely waiting out a winter storm, safe in the south of England.

"Do you think me a failure, Mr. Loxley?" Thorncress asked suddenly.

"What? No, sir! I never thought any such thing."

"I've tried my utmost to do right by you. I've tried to keep your spirits up." His voice was low, as if he were speaking to himself, and Loxley's proximity was mere happenstance. "But the truth of the matter is that Faerie wins, every time. It takes and it takes and it takes, and there is little us mortals can do but try to bear it." He kept his gaze fixed on the yard beyond the window, even as Loxley stared at him agape.

"You have done more than your duty to me," Loxley managed, putting his hand on Thorncress' arm. His muscles were coiled tight under his coat, like he meant to pull himself away, though he didn't move. His stillness seemed painful. "Were the creature to steal me away tomorrow, I could hold nothing against you. Your efforts have been far above and beyond what any man could expect of a stranger met on the moors, and regardless of the ending, I owe you everything. You cannot think otherwise."

Thorncress offered him a grim smile. "You're a good man, Loxley. You deserve better than this."

"Perhaps, but so do you," Loxley returned stubbornly. "Come away from the window. If we're to stay here another day or two, let's not spend them brooding. I'll put the kettle on. This weather calls for tea."

Thorncress allowed himself to be led back to the bed and pushed down onto it while Loxley busied himself in the kitchen, trying to ignore the anxiety gnawing at his insides. Thorncress had always been so solid: in his convictions, in every action and decision. Loxley didn't know what to make of his sudden turn to melancholy. Or perhaps not melancholy, for that seemed a dull and drowning mood, and Thorncress radiated a dark and foreboding resignation.

Bringing the kettle to the fireplace, Loxley thought that perhaps the distinction mattered little.

❊ ❊ ❊

As morning passed into afternoon and the sun tracked its wan path across the sky, seen only in glimpses from between the clouds, they took to the yard again. The snow had gentled, settling powdery on the ground, and Loxley sent it spraying up in glittering arcs as he walked. It was ghostly silent amid the trees, and strangely peaceful.

"I was happy, here." He pressed his hand to the great hawthorn as if greeting an old friend, though their familiarity had withered and grown distant. "I played here for years, and then I forgot it all so easily when I left. Perhaps, if I had remembered it better, I wouldn't have been caught so easily."

"No use contemplating what might have been. But, for what it's worth, I'm glad you were happy then."

Kneeling, Loxley cleared away the snow near the base of the trunk. The dancing figure was still visible, a white scar in the wood amid the scorch marks Loxley had inflicted. Would it have made a difference if he'd tried to burn it away as a child? Or if he had never acknowledged it at all, never spoken to it or shared his name?

He sat down in the snow, heedless of the cold, and wrapped his arms around his knees, staring at the patterns in the bark.

"I thought that the longer we fought this thing, the more my fear would fade, if only into exhaustion." His throat threatened to close with a strangled sob; he choked it down again. "But it comes in waves. They hit me unexpectedly, sometimes when I thought I had accepted my fate, or even sometimes when optimism had wrestled back control— I've never felt fear like this. I don't know what to do."

"Fear for your soul?"

"I've feared for that often enough. This feels like a child's fear of the dark, that instinctive flinch from the unknown. I've heard enough stories of Hell, but Faerie?" He curled in tighter. "I don't know. Will it hurt to cross over? It's akin to death, and I cannot stop my fear of dying."

"I cannot reassure you. I wish I could."

Loxley shook his head and forced himself to his feet, brushing the snow from his coat and trousers. "I apologize. There are few men who don't fear death. If I didn't have to face it now, I would have to make my peace with it later. It's quite inevitable." He glanced at Thorncress, a ragged black shape against the snow, like a crow. "But you made your peace years ago, didn't you? Chasing the hounds, as you do."

"I thought I had."

"Teach me how?"

Before Thorncress could reply, something moved in the woods. Loxley felt rather than saw it: some primal instinct in him sharpened and stood to attention, all his senses trained to the darkness beyond the trees. For a second, heavy silence hung—

And then the snow was pierced by a long, wavering cry that shocked Loxley to his core. His hairs all stood on end and he was rooted to the spot, eyes wide and mouth open, about to speak but unable to interrupt that unearthly wail. Beside him, Thorncress' gaze was far away, his stare stricken, and that, more than the cry itself, urged Loxley to action. He pulled his scarf free from his throat and lunged for Thorncress, bearing them both to the ground in a frantic tangle of limbs. Pinning him down, Loxley covered his eyes with the scarf before burying his face in Thorncress' coat. Thorncress' breath was hot against his hair, and though his hands came up to grasp Loxley's shoulders, he made no attempt to throw him off.

"Don't look," Loxley begged, his voice muffled from being pressed to Thorncress' chest where he lay atop him. "I know I said that your business was your own, but I couldn't bear it if you left me now. Please, don't look for the hounds."

"It's alright." Thorncress' voice was choked, but Loxley didn't dare lift his head to see what expression he wore. "I didn't look. My eyes are shut, and I won't open them."

"And the next time they come? Will you shut your eyes again, or will you throw your life away to keep a decades-old promise to the dead?"

"Loxley—"

"Is there anything in this world that could keep you here?"

Thorncress went still beneath him, his hands frozen on Loxley's waist. "My family is gone. Who else is left to mourn me?"

The scarf twisted in Loxley's hands, digging into Thorncress' cheeks deeply enough to leave a mark. "I would mourn you," he hissed. The words came dragged from his lips like a confession, ragged and stinging in their honesty. "If you've ever felt anything for me whatsoever, you will not do this. Please." He pulled in a breath. "I love you. I hadn't meant to say so, knowing your intent to follow the hounds, but now that we're here, I can't let you go. My heart won't take it. I don't care if you think me weak—if I can stop you from following them, I will." On the last word, his voice gave out, and he dug his teeth into his lip until he tasted blood.

Thorncress moved his hands from Loxley's waist to his back, crushing him close. "I don't think you weak. I never did."

He stilled, his body tense, and Loxley waited.

The hounds came out of the woods.

Loxley heard them approach on snowy paws, panting in the cold. They spoke to one another in musical voices, their words dog-shaped. Their presence drew nearer, until they were so close that he could feel their hot breath on the back of his neck. Whiskers grazed his naked skin where his scarf wasn't, and he flinched and curled his shoulders in, trying to hide.

"They won't hurt you," Thorncress said, "so long as you don't look."

"I won't look," Loxley promised through gritted teeth.

A cold, wet nose pressed against the back of his hand where he held the scarf against Thorncress' face. His heart beat rabbit-fast and he held his breath to keep from making a sound. Did the hounds think of him as prey? He waited to feel sharp teeth dig into him, but none came. Instead, after a few seconds of being nudged by that nose—the hound's muzzle was impossibly soft, its touch gentle—a warm tongue ran over his knuckles. It lasted only an instant, and then it was gone. The hounds spoke again, and turned to lope off through the yard, raising their cry once more.

Loxley and Thorncress stayed where they were long after the last sounds of the hounds had faded. The snow built up on Loxley's back and in his hair, but he didn't move. He could only focus on the rhythm of Thorncress' breath, and the gradual synchronization of their hearts.

"They're gone," Thorncress finally said.

Loxley stirred. His fingers had gone numb around the scarf, he had clenched it so tightly. "If I take this away, will you chase them?"

Slowly, Thorncress lifted one hand to push the scarf aside, and Loxley let him, opening his eyes for the first time. The sky had darkened from afternoon to the purgatory that came before dusk. Thorncress' hair was splayed out against the snow, and flakes settled in to land on his eyelashes and melt against his lips. He looked as if Loxley had driven a knife between his ribs rather than simply blindfolded him, and he lay perfectly still. "I will not chase them," he said haltingly, wetting his lips. "I had not realized you felt . . ." He cleared his throat and glanced away. "I hadn't realized the depth of the friendship you offered."

Loxley bit out a laugh, more shock than humour. "The depth? Sir, I let you bed me! I'm not—I've never—" He blushed hotly, despite the snow. "I care for you. Deeply, yes. And I would not have you leave me in such a careless manner as this. Not when we can both avoid it. You know how it feels to be left behind. You must have more compassion than that."

"I apologize," Thorncress said hoarsely. "On several counts. But I swear, I will not chase the hounds."

Loxley rose in stiff increments, clambering off him and wrapping the scarf back around his neck. Thorncress followed him up, not quite meeting his eye. Hesitantly, Loxley took his hand. "I love you, and I would miss you, if you went. I need you to know that."

Thorncress made a quiet sound like a wounded animal. "I cannot promise what will happen come morning," he said, his throat working furiously, "but I will not leave you tonight. Wherever the hounds went, I won't follow. You have my word." Raising one hand, he traced the trail of tears from Loxley's eye to the line of his jaw. "Don't cry for me. Please."

"I will cry for you," Loxley threatened, though he managed a shaky smile. "I'll cry for you every night and every day until you realize the depth of my feelings for you." He dropped his gaze to the place where he held Thorncress' hand. "I thought the love you bore for her was worth your life, but what of my love for you? Is that not worth something, too?"

"It is." No tears welled in Thorncress' eyes, but his touch was gentle as he tucked Loxley's errant curls behind one ear.

Closing his eyes, Loxley leaned into the touch. "Can we go inside now? We may talk more there, or in the morning, but I should very much like to warm up by the fire." His eyes flickered open and he glanced at Thorncress through his lashes. "With you," he added. "I would like to lay with you and keep you in arm's reach. In case I have been unclear."

"You're clear enough," Thorncress murmured. "But must we talk?"

"It was a lack of talk that led us here," Loxley said pointedly, drawing back to look him in the eye. "We shall talk until I'm convinced that you're not going to throw your life away. I want you to stay, if not with me, then at least—"

"I will not die in the night," Thorncress promised. "Nor in three day's-time."

"Not then, either."

Loxley took a deep breath. "Very well. It's a start." It was a ridiculous thing to promise, of course: no man could guarantee such a thing with any certainty. "Inside." He tugged on Thorncress' hand. "We'll catch cold if we stand out here much longer."

Thorncress brushed himself free of snow, then did the same for Loxley. He ruffled the snowflakes free from Loxley's curls, swept them from his shoulders and off his back. Loxley shivered, both from the attention and the lingering memory of the hounds. His hand still felt hot where the hound had licked it, tingling with raw nerves.

"You're alright," Thorncress said, taking the hand in question to draw him back to the house.

"It didn't hurt me. It felt like an apology, somehow."

Thorncress blew out his breath in a gust of snow. "Come on. Let's get you warmed up."

Inside, they undressed each other with frozen fingers, hanging their clothes to dry before wrapping themselves in the covers to perch on the edge of the bed, as close to the fire as they could manage. They ate dinner like that, shoulder to shoulder and thigh to thigh, huddled under the blankets until they were warm again. Loxley memorized the lines of Thorncress' face: the circles under his eyes, the sweep of his eyelashes and the dark arch of his eyebrows, how his hair always escaped its tie to fall over his shoulders in rough waves. It lent him a romantic look: windswept and dark-featured, the firelight reflected in his eyes and dancing over his sienna skin. His stubble had grown heavier over the past days. It would grow into a proper beard soon enough, but

Loxley liked it in between. He pressed a kiss to Thorncress' jaw just because he could, both of them cradling mugs of tea in their hands. It was the most intimate Loxley had ever been with anyone, just sitting in each other's space. He could scarcely believe he was allowed to look, let alone touch and taste. Whatever he wanted, Thorncress gave him, meeting him halfway in every act and then taking him further. Every kiss Loxley offered, Thorncress returned, as with every touch, embrace, and stroke.

"I would stay like this forever, if I could," Loxley said against Thorncress' skin. "I wish I had found you earlier. I wish I could have had this years ago." For though the creature had not yet taken him, it was only a matter of time. His days were numbered, and the grief at what he was about to lose was smothering. "I'm glad I have you. I don't think I could bear it, were I alone in all of this."

"You would find a way."

Loxley kissed his knuckles, deliberately looking away from the concern etched in Thorncress' brow. "No. Not now that I know what I would be missing."

※ ※ ※

He only woke once in the night, to the feeling of Thorncress pressed close to his back like a shell.

"I didn't think I would ever find love," Thorncress murmured, his face nuzzled against the nape of Loxley's neck. "I'm too much my mother's son. I know what people see when they look at me, and I don't make myself an easy companion. I didn't think . . ."

"It's alright," Loxley said, half-asleep. "I see you."

Thorncress pressed a hot, closed-mouth kiss to the junction of Loxley's body where neck met shoulder.

"Sleep," Loxley coaxed. "We'll talk in the morning."

Thorncress said nothing, only ducked his head and held him tighter, and Loxley fell asleep in his arms.

※ ※ ※

Dawn broke cold and sterile. The sunlight that filtered through the window was more grey than gold, and the fire had burned itself out sometime in the night. Thorncress had donned his shirt and trousers again and retreated to his side of the mattress while Loxley slept, though Loxley didn't anticipate an early start to their day. Turning onto his back, he intended to luxuriate in bed for some time. The snow had piled high through the night, though it was no longer falling, and he had no great desire to go out and encounter the creature again, or worse still, the hounds.

But a prickle of unease crept over him. It began in his fingertips and crawled up his arms to the back of his neck, and shivered there like a bad omen. The room's chill slunk under the covers to settle into the marrow of his bones. Beside him, the mattress was cold.

As slowly as he dared, he turned to face Thorncress, who did not stir as he normally would. His sleep-soft smile and rough-voiced *good morning* were absent. The silence was suffocating.

"Thorncress?" Loxley whispered. He reached out to touch the shoulder nearest him. "John?"

CHAPTER ELEVEN

THE GRAVE BENEATH THE HAWTHORN

Loxley dug the grave beneath the hawthorn tree. The ground was frozen, the ice having clawed its way deep into the earth, yet he was numb to the blisters that rubbed his palms raw, and the cold sweat that clung to his chest and the small of his back. He dug until the sun hung overhead, and when the grave was deep enough, he rolled the body in.

Clasping his hands over the shovel's handle, he tipped his face to the sky. For a moment, he could do nothing but breathe: great, shuddering breaths like he was drowning, as the pale sun blinked down at him, and wispy clouds streaked the sky, broken by the black, spindly fingers of the trees. Thorncress' eyes were closed as if he slept still, his face blank of all expression. He had not died afraid, at least, but that offered Loxley little comfort.

"Dear God," he began, but his voice splintered, and he broke off. He had nothing to say, no prayers to offer, and besides which, Thorncress had turned from God long ago.

Dropping his gaze back to Thorncress' body, Loxley found he had nothing to say to him, either. He had no flowers to bury with him, though he doubted Thorncress had much use for such sentiments. A single rose, perhaps, laid upon his breast, in memory of his sister. Hesitating, he finally tore the rowan charm free from his coat, dropping it into the grave where it settled over Thorncress' heart. He had no more use for it, but perhaps the protection of the rowan wood would cancel out the faerie influence of the hawthorn tree and safeguard Thorncress, small as it was.

Whatever was left of him to safeguard.

Loxley pushed his hair back from his forehead, and, bending his back to the task, piled the dirt back in. He kept his gaze averted so as not to see the moment when it covered Thorncress' face. It would have been easier with a coffin. He swallowed a dry sob.

When it was done, the dirt raised high in a bed, he stared at the hawthorn's gnarled trunk that served as Thorncress' headstone. If the sun offered any warmth, he couldn't feel it. The wind, cold and biting, whispered over him, nipping at his cheeks and leaving his skin chapped, but he only felt hollow. Like someone had reached inside him as he slept and plucked out his heart to bury in the cold, dark earth, and he hadn't noticed until it was too late.

He stood until the cold burned his lungs and he lost all feeling in his body, and then he stood there longer still. Finally, when his legs threatened to fold under him, he turned and laid one hand against the tree.

"If you remember me with any love, watch over him. Wrap him in your roots and keep the animals and insects at bay. Keep him safe."

He picked his way through the yard to the house without looking back. The bed lay cold and empty; the hearth, the same. Thorncress' coat lay draped over the back of one chair, and Loxley hesitated before picking it up. It still smelled like him, like bonfire smoke and cinnamon oranges, and Loxley lifted it to his face to breathe it in before examining the contents of its pockets. It held Thorncress' wallet, containing a handful of coins, his knife, his pipe and a flask, and, in the inner breast pocket, an envelope so old that the paper was worn soft. The tattered remains of a seal still clung to it, and the ink that spelled out Thorncress' name had faded—*John*, the letters gently curling—but was still strong. Twenty years ago, Rosa Thorncress had seen the hounds, and bid her brother farewell on paper. Now, he had followed her, but left no letter in his wake. Loxley slipped the envelope back into its pocket and pulled the coat over his shoulders, wrapping himself in Thorncress' scent. He wasn't brave enough to read that letter and see what Rosa had made of her fate. Not yet.

He moved as if sleepwalking, his limbs performing the necessary actions to move him from one place to another without any direction from his mind. He had always imagined that grief would feel like a raw wound, or a storm breaking, but he felt more like he had lain down in the heathers the previous night and woken to find that the snow had covered him, weighing him down. Like a man succumbing to the sleep of hypothermia, he couldn't rouse himself from under that blanket of snow. If he fought his way out, perhaps feeling would return to his body—but so too would the pain, and the realization that Thorncress was gone. He had grieved his parents' deaths, but there had been time to prepare for those. He had mourned their passing, but the experience hadn't crushed him. Not like this heavy snow-grief would crush him.

He collected the horses and rode for Scarborough. The road was longer than he remembered, yet the journey passed in no time at all. He watched the sky shift and sway; the clouds chased each other from one horizon to the other, and the sun gleamed down in faint rays, only visible for a moment at a time. The watercolour sky deepened to an oil painting as the day wore on, turning yellow and charcoal grey, devouring the faint snatches of blue like they had never existed. The north had not always been so relentlessly grey, and not so cold, either. He felt like he was watching the scenery roll past from someone else's eyes.

Grace Blackburn's house was as they had left it, standing solitarily on the edge of town, guarded by her broad-crowned rowan tree. Loxley knocked on the door just once, the wood harsh against his knuckles. A single knell, like the toll of a death bell. Then he waited, his breath pluming ghostly in the winter air.

Ms. Blackburn gazed past him as she opened the door, her pale, twin pupils reflecting the darkening sky. "Mr. Loxley?"

He forced himself to speak, though his tongue was leaden and his throat asphyxiated. "You knew what he meant to do."

She went terribly still, one hand clasped on the doorframe.

"I heard you talking, that night. You knew he meant to follow the hounds. To follow her."

"I knew."

"He promised he wouldn't leave me."

"Mr. Loxley . . ."

He shook his head abruptly, wiping the sting of tears from his eyes. "No matter. The end result is the same. Whether Faerie took him first or second, it was always going to have us both, in the end. You know better than anyone the futility of questioning its will."

"Will you come inside, Mr. Loxley? Sit, and tell me what happened."

Her voice faltered, and he was distantly aware that she had lost a friend, as well.

"I have no story to tell," he said weakly. "The hounds came, as they do. He swore he never saw them, that he wouldn't look, for my sake if not for his, but I woke up this morning and he did not. Forgive me. You knew him longer, and you deserve to know more than that, but I can't . . . I have nothing more to offer. I only came to tell you that he is gone, and to return your charm."

Pulling the cross free of its cord, he held it out to her. His chest was cold without its familiar weight against his collarbones, but then, his whole body was cold. His heart ached from the frost.

When she didn't accept it, he took her wrist and turned her hand palm up, pressing it in and closing her fingers around it. They both ignored the burn.

"Mr. Loxley, I cannot take this back. Without it—"

"I know. But there's no point in going on without him, is there? It will only be a matter of time before the creature finds me again, charm or not, and without him . . ."

She clasped his hand between both of hers. "Mr. Loxley, this is a death wish."

"Then I'll be in good company."

Withdrawing his hand, he searched Thorncress' pockets for the remains of their worldly goods. "Here— take this as well. There's a little money left from both of us. I have no need of it, and it seems a shame to let it go to waste." He hesitated. "And his knife, if you like. Something to remember him by."

"This is madness. You'll not even take a weapon to defend yourself?"

He smiled forlornly. "I can't kill it. I hadn't even the heart to fell a tree."

"I can't accept these things," she said firmly. "You're grieving. Sleep here tonight—you'll look on things more clearly come morning."

Loxley blanched at the thought of spending the night in the same bed where he and Thorncress had first touched, and Ms. Blackburn must have sensed it, for she quickly added, "Or take a room at an inn, and join me tomorrow. We can talk. We can—"

"Please," he interrupted. "Please, Ms. Blackburn—I can't. Either take these things, or I'll bury them." *And myself*, he didn't say. "I'll leave my horse in town under your name; you may sell him, if you wish. And his horse, too, though I must first take him further north. I only wanted to say thank you, for everything you did for us—for him. Because I think you tried to talk him out of chasing the hounds more than once, though he was too stubborn to listen. And that I'm sorry . . ." He swallowed. "I'm sorry for your loss."

She turned the charm over in her hands, leaving red marks in its wake. "I did try to stop him. I had thought, with you by his side, perhaps that would be enough to tether him to this world. But Faerie will take as it pleases."

"Did it take him? Or did he give himself to it?"

"The claim it laid on him was more insidious than yours or mine, but just as inevitable." She smiled sadly and touched Loxley's face. Her palm was warm, and he shut his eyes as he leaned into it. "I'm sorry, Mr. Loxley. You're a good man, and you deserve a better end than this."

"So did he," he said brokenly. "Do you know what will happen to me?"

She shook her head. "I don't know, and cannot say. They split my eyes, one pupil for each world, and blinded me to both."

He nodded, his gaze on the frost-bitten ground. "We were staying at my old house, in Pickering, at the edge of Dalby Forest. He's buried in the back yard with your rowan charm, beneath the hawthorn tree. It seemed a fitting gravestone, all things considered, but there was no coffin. If you wish to visit him, or if you know somewhere better suited . . ."

"Thank you."

"I won't be seeing you again, I don't think."

"No," she said quietly, "I don't expect you will. Goodbye, Mr. Loxley, and God be with you."

He turned away, into the ever-darkening twilight. "He's not."

Without the charm's protection, the sun seemed weaker, and the ground was so very hard under his boots. He couldn't imagine being a body buried beneath it.

He rode north until the woods thinned and the crunch of leaves underfoot turned to heather, and the sky opened up wide and unbroken. A great expanse of nothingness. The early evening stars were crystalline and perfectly untouchable in the grey. He rode until everything seemed alien and strange, yet achingly familiar: the moors, that desolate place where Thorncress made his home. The place where Loxley had always felt most insignificant, and the most overwhelmed by the bare beauty of the land.

He halted only when the faerie tree appeared, a gnarled and twisted shape jutting out from the horizon.

There he dismounted, tying the horse's reins out of the way, and let him go. They hadn't gone so very far from Scarborough; the horse would find his way back without trouble. He had been born and bred on the moors as surely as Thorncress had.

Picking his way through the heather, Loxley made for the tree, the lone sign of life in the barren landscape, and in its shelter, sat down upon its gnarled roots to wait. The earth was awash in the strange half-light of dusk: one last breath of light before the coming dark. The stars watched him with neither sympathy nor reproach, slowly spinning. The galaxies would join them soon in the dark, but Loxley doubted he would have to wait that long. He had brought no food, no water, and no protection. His mouth was dry and his stomach empty, but neither bothered him. As he watched the clouds streak across the horizon like birds winging their way home to nest, the letter weighed heavily against his heart, and finally, he withdrew the envelope and slipped it free.

Dear John,

The snow is beautiful here: the yard is painted in glitter and diamonds, and every tree seems made of glass. Our parents are in good health and spirits, despite the cold, and Ma has already begun talking of your return come spring.

But, dearest John, I must ask you to return early, though I know the roads are nigh impassible now.

I saw the hounds this morning. I haven't told our parents, for I can't bear the thought of filling our last days together with such sadness. I'm sorry that I won't see you again before I go. Please don't blame me for it—I was stacking firewood in the yard when I heard their song, and I looked before I could stop myself. Their music is so stirring, voices fit for Heaven—except that they seem to predate Heaven, as if they're older than God Himself, like the deities we worshipped before Christianity ever took root. You may chastise me for such blasphemy, but I am already cut off from Heaven, and no amount of prayer or atonement will gain me entrance. If I cannot blaspheme now, then when?

They are more beautiful and terrible than the stories say. Greater than any mortal hound I've ever seen, with fur as white as snow, and pale eyes with such awful knowledge in them. Gazing on them, I was struck by the idea that they held the fate of each and every one of us in their teeth, and that my death had been written long before I was ever born, and the hounds were here only to enact it. It was as if my seeing them were inevitable, for when I looked on them, the world made sense again in ways I haven't felt since I was a child.

I entreat you, do not cry for me, nor blame the hounds, though I know you will do both. Better to believe that some invisible illness in my blood struck me down unawares. I will not say that I am not afraid, for though I have accepted my death, I don't know whether I can face it bravely. I only hope that when my time comes, wherever my soul goes, I might hear the hounds sing again.

Take care, and may God be with you, since He is no longer with me. I love you with all my heart.

Ever yours,
Rosa

Loxley stared at the letter long after he finished reading it. Had Thorncress felt that same spark of recognition upon seeing the hounds? Had he too understood the nature of fate and death and inevitability, in a way that Loxley, who had never borne witness, could not?

But he had heard their call, and saw his own reaction to it reflected in Rosa's long-dead words. Older than Heaven and older than God.

He folded the letter back into its original shape, tucking it inside the envelope and returning it to the breast pocket of Thorncress' coat where it had lived for decades, over his heart. He should have buried it alongside Thorncress. Reading it had only made the ache in his own heart worsen. Folding his hands over his knee to keep from trembling, he watched the sky, and waited.

When Loxley's shadow was lost to the last, lingering rays of the dying sun, the creature appeared. It came out from behind the hawthorn, taking shape slowly, as if its physical form needed to be gathered from the air around it. Loxley saw it from the corner of his eye, and forced his gaze ahead, not turning until it was in full view. Creeping forward on all fours, it stopped some yards away from Loxley, and stared at him with keen, luminous eyes.

"Alone this time," it said, its voice like a branch scratching at the windowpane.

"Do you still need me to open your door?"

It slunk forward another inch. "My door . . ."

"John Thorncress is dead, and I mean to follow him. Tell me what I need to do."

"My door," the creature repeated, its voice strengthening. "You will be my door. It will not hurt much, no, make it good, I . . ."

"I'll do it, if it will take my soul to Faerie."

The creature nodded emphatically, close enough to touch, though Loxley did not recoil. "Put you to sleep." Its breath was a cool gust against Loxley's skin, like winter wind. "Put you to sleep and the door opens up around you, through you, and when *they* come through to take their gift, slip through, I."

"And I?" Loxley asked, his heart beating staccato in his chest.

"Dead," the creature affirmed, "dead and gone, to dust, to leaves, to soil."

"And my soul?" he pressed.

"In Faerie," the creature promised, its hands like claws on Loxley's knees. "It passes into Faerie, beautiful Faerieland, where cold is no more. All summer gold and leaves in the trees, flowers to bloom, dripping honey. No more cold, no more winter, no more grinding teeth or tears. Only birdsong and dancing and warm summer sun. Yes? To Faerie? You open the door?"

Loxley nodded, his tongue thick. "I'll do it. Only—please—make it quick."

The creature nodded again, climbing up on its knees to run its hands up his thighs, scratching him through his trousers in its eagerness. Loxley flinched back and it smoothed its palms down in supplication. "Quick as a mouse, quick as birdsong. Quick for my pretty prince, quick and scarcely any pain at all. Dead and gone, leaves and soil . . ."

Its touch was freezing, but Loxley clenched his jaw and held his ground. He was too hollow for fear and too resolved to entertain second thoughts. No time for regret, not with Thorncress already dead and buried beneath the snow. He had been dead nigh on twelve hours, if he had died at dawn. Loxley took comfort in the thought that at least he had not slept long in that bed beside his corpse. But it was said that time in Faerie moved differently, and with every passing moment, Thorncress was slipping further and further away. A thousand years could have passed already.

"Do it," Loxley said. "Enchant me. Put me to sleep."

The creature grinned like a shark and lunged up, one hand tangling in Loxley's hair and the other grasping his jaw to hold him in place as it crushed its cold, blue lips to his. The kiss was aggressive and over-eager, all teeth and feral enthusiasm, and Loxley's eyes were wide in shock as he sat paralyzed under the force of it. The creature climbed into his lap, weighing no more than skin and bones. It emanated chill from every point of contact, a stark contrast to the solid, heavy warmth that Thorncress' body had been—but Loxley couldn't think of that. He forced his eyes closed and put his hands on the creature's narrow shoulders, even as he tasted the sharp tang of blood on his tongue. It flooded his mouth, thick and hot, and though his eyes flew open and he tried to pull back to spit it out, the creature followed him, grinning wildly even as it nipped at his mouth, his jaw, his throat, whatever it could reach.

"So sweet," it crooned, stroking his face in too-quick movements. "My sweet summertime boy, like plums and peaches, strawberries and cream . . ."

Loxley pushed the creature back to wipe the blood from his lips, but the creature just licked its own, staring back at him in rapture. Its teeth were stained red.

"The enchantment?" Loxley asked.

"Beginning now. Soon you sleep. Sleep, warm, not to wake again. Peaceful. Body dies when the mind is already gone: no more pain. No more than this." It reached out a long, thin finger. The nail was sharp and long and pale like a diamond, and stopped just short of touching Loxley's face. "Hurts?"

"Yes. A little."

"But not much." The creature nodded to itself, seemingly satisfied. "Promise kept." It inched forward again. "Another taste, before you go? Just a little bit, a little bite, the smallest kiss—"

This time when it captured his lips, Loxley was prepared. He swallowed the rush of metallic blood and breathed through his nose as the creature explored him: inside, its tongue, as cool as the rest of it; outside, its hands, roaming over his shoulders and up and down his sides like it had never touched another being before. Maybe it hadn't, or at least, not in a very long time. It hurt to contemplate such a lonely existence, so similar to his own.

"So sweet, so warm," the creature murmured, running its hands through his hair and turning his head this way and that, as if searching for something in Loxley's eyes, illuminated by the last reach of the sun.

Loxley didn't know what his eyes showed; all he felt was a terrible, all-encompassing weariness, and a chill that ached him to the bones. Somewhere on the other side of that wall of exhaustion there was grief—the wild kind, so heavy one could drown in it—but he couldn't feel that yet. Maybe, if the creature enchanted him just so, he wouldn't have to.

"Do you feel it?" the creature asked, its pale eyes staring deep into Loxley's. Its nails dug into his shoulders. "Feel it coming?"

"I feel tired."

"Good. Tired. Come, come down, down to the earth . . ."

The creature took his hands and coaxed him from his seat of tree roots to kneel amid the darkening heather. Loxley could barely keep his eyes open; was this how it had been before, before he had forgotten?

"Forget," the creature soothed, stroking his face tenderly. "Forget, soon, and sleep. Deep rest. No more hurt. Yes?"

"Yes," Loxley said, though no sound came out. His voice was a dry and brittle thing trapped somewhere in his chest, like dead leaves rattling in the wind. He lay down carefully on his side, curling to pillow one elbow beneath his head. It wasn't comfortable, but neither was he conscious of the discomfort. He simply was.

"My sweet boy," the creature murmured, petting his hair. "Here you rest, and I draw the ring around. Then we wait, honey in the trap, for those sweet-voiced flies to come buzzing in and open up the road between the worlds. Cannot resist coming to those who call. So curious. So vain." It pressed a lingering kiss to Loxley's temple, and that one didn't hurt at all. "Then hand in hand your soul and I slip through, and the wild summerlands embrace us, long lost children. Free from this cold. Such frost, such never-ending snow. Do you not tire of it? The long dark of winter? Endless rains? Better on the other side. Shouldn't have waited so long. Could have seen it all . . ."

Loxley let his eyes fall shut as he tuned out the creature's aimless chatter. Though the ground was hard with frost, his body seemed to sink into it, as if into a bed of moss or soft, rich soil. He imagined Thorncress in the ground beneath him, waiting for him to make his way down.

No grave for Loxley, though: no hymns or eulogies. Not even a friend to stand over his body and see him gone. He would die, as he had lived, a heathen. He let his body sink further into the heather's embrace. Around him, a ring of mushrooms poked up through the earth, their stalks slender and breakable at first, their caps small and delicate.

"Soon," the creature whispered. "Our time, so soon. The door cracks open and we slip through with dawn's first light."

"Dawn?"

The creature lay down behind him, curling close in a rough imitation of how Thorncress had once lain, and put its arm around him and tugged him close. Its mouth was cold against his neck. "Dawn is not so far. Sleep, my prince. Sweet prince, honey prince. Sleep."

It kissed him, biting tiny marks into his shoulders, stroking up and down his side as if to keep him warm, and Loxley drifted under. With every touch of the creature's skin against his own it grew harder to keep his eyes open or his mind afloat, and too soon, the dreams came rushing to the surface and dragged him down. The last thing he knew was the creature's cold presence at his back, and its nonsense whispering in his ear, like the sweet nothings of an idle lover. Thorncress never wasted words like that, but Thorncress was . . . He was . . .

Loxley took one last conscious breath, the heather brushing his lips like the earth itself were offering a kiss, and then the enchantment took hold the rest of the way and he was gone.

CHAPTER TWELVE

THE DOOR TO FAERIE

Loxley woke with the dawn, and for one terrible moment, he thought the enchantment had been broken. But no, Thorncress was dead, and there was no one else to rescue him. The mushrooms had grown tall through the night, their sturdy brown caps poking up to stand above the heather. Besides which, Loxley still felt enchanted, like a heavy gauze was hung around him, keeping him slow and drowsy. The sun was pale on the horizon, a yellow light that barely broke through the wall of grey. The door had not yet opened: of that, he was certain.

Sitting up, his body was stiff and slow to obey, whether from the enchantment or from the previous day's work, he didn't know. He sat cross-legged, his hands on his knees, and tipped his face toward the rising sun to wait.

It had snowed again overnight; the ground was dusted with it, as was his person. He let it melt from his hair without making any effort to brush it away. It wouldn't matter soon. Already Loxley felt untethered from the world, though perhaps that was only grief.

He swallowed it down. He couldn't grieve, because Thorncress wasn't lost to him. Was this how Thorncress had felt for twenty years since his Rosa died? Loxley regretted having ever begged him to stay. Faerie hounds, indeed—and then Loxley had turned and delivered himself to his creature.

"What a pair we make." His lips were cracked, dry and split deep, both from the cold and from the creature's kisses. It was a distant pain, like the cold and the blisters, and easily ignored. "I hope you found her." His words were barely more than a breath. They made a little plume of ice crystals in the air as they left his lungs. "I'm coming. I'm so close. You told me to look for Faerie in the sky, behind the clouds, but it's closer than that. It's all around me. If I stood, I feel I could reach out and touch it even now."

Something shivered in the corner of his eye, but when he turned to look, there was nothing. He exhaled just to see his breath—still alive, but barely—and shut his eyes to count down from ten.

When he opened them again, the world was changing.

The heather swayed as if blown by a wild gust, and the sky shimmered like gossamer. Behind him, the hawthorn tree creaked and groaned, its branches budding before his eyes, tiny apples bursting into bloom like drops of blood from an open wound. Loxley pressed both hands to the earth and felt it shudder, like a great beast waking in the planet's core, yet his body did not shake where he sat. The clouds rolled in strange shapes and the sun brightened between one blink and the next, from pale yellow to bright gold.

Loxley held his breath.

In a flash, everything pitched sideways, sharp and sudden, and he fell to the ground. Something above him lunged with a snarl, teeth stained red—the creature? But it was too large for that, with too many limbs, and a hundred thousand insect wings that glittered, iridescent, on its back—and a rush of skin and fur and beetle armour and the smell of roses under the year's first frost—

The sky went dark and the breath froze in his lungs, and he knew no more.

※ ※ ※

The first thing he noticed was the warmth. Summer sun beat down on his face, like he had fallen asleep midday in the conservatory. His body woke before his mind, and he basked in that warmth for an indeterminate time. The ground beneath him was soft, and the gentle trill of birdsong filled the air and set his heart at ease.

But I was on the moors, he thought, and abruptly his mind broke through the pleasant haze, and he opened his eyes and sat up.

He was still on the moors, or a place much like them. The moors as imagined by a romantic who had never seen them in person, perhaps. The heather was a rich, deep purple, undaunted by the snow, the sky more blue than grey, and the sun was brighter, like a coin made of molten gold. The birdsong that had sounded so sweet a moment ago dropped away as he realized that there was no tree but the barren hawthorn in which a bird might perch to sing.

"Have I passed through?" he asked aloud. He had never dared imagine Faerie, but he had hoped that Thorncress would be waiting for him, as on the other side of a door. Thorncress had always waited for him before. The disappointment stung in his chest, but he pushed it aside and struggled to his feet. He had not yet consciously cried, and he did not wish to start.

The sky was painted with the dawn, but not the pale winter dawns with which he was familiar. Rather, it was the sunrise he remembered from his childhood, when the sun touched the summer wildflowers outside his window and turned them bright and vivid, and bathed his room in pools of buttery gold.

Standing, he took stock of himself. He was clothed in the same outfit in which he had fallen asleep, Thorncress' coat heavy on his shoulders, yet the fabric felt light and clean against his skin, and his body was not as stiff or sore as he had expected, after sleeping on the ground. There was still heather beneath his feet, and behind him stood the lonesome hawthorn. But this land was not England, and these were not the moors.

"Awake," said a bright voice, and Loxley spun to face it.

The creature stood before him, upright like a man, though it could never pass as such. Its skin was still too pale, but rather than the cold, deathly grey it had worn before, it seemed to shimmer like an opal in the sun, and it moved with far more grace than the creeping, slinking thing it had been in England. Shapes that may have been wings flickered at its back, insectoid and glittering like those of a great beetle or a dragonfly. They did not seem inclined to solidify for long enough for Loxley to determine their nature with any more accuracy than that.

"We have passed through the door and walked down the road," the creature said. Here, in the sun, it sounded different too: less of a scratching whisper, fuller and livelier.

"Is this your true form?" Loxley tugged on the buttons of Thorncress' coat; he had not expected to take it with him; he had scarcely expected to wake with a physical form at all. "Is this mine?"

"No, neither. You are human still, human soul, human mind. Cannot comprehend true fae. Why the land still looks like yours." The creature smiled widely. Its teeth looked the same—still small and terribly sharp, and still stained red from Loxley's blood. "Will look less so, the further in you go. Forget England: find Faerie. Then perhaps you see my true form."

"What does it look like?"

"Beautiful. Terrible."

The creature stretched and preened, and the shapes that could be wings flared out behind it like vast, flickering shadows. For an instant Loxley saw a second form imposed on the first, as if painted atop a sheet of transparent film: something huge and long and lean, with too many limbs and faces—and then the creature settled and it was gone.

"Went so long without it," the creature said wistfully. "Earth, mortal eyes—crammed into such a small body. Left for dead. Here, I remember myself again."

"How did you come to be locked out of Faerie for so long?"

"Born sickly, I. Faerie stole a human child and left me in its place, unwanted."

"But you didn't die."

The creature shook its head. "New parents, the mortals, they knew. Recognized me for the cuckoo egg I was."

"The Cobbs?" Loxley hazarded. "Thomas and Anna?"

The creature broke into a wide grin. "Thomas and Anna, yes, they called me Cobb. Scared of what might happen if they cast me out, they nursed me back to health like I was their own. Disguised as a human babe, frost and ice I was. Cobbs kept me alive. Grew better. Stronger. I repaid them with silver and gold, shiny things, furs and stones, good health and long, long life. They were happy for it. No debt to them. Dead, now. Dead and gone. And I, alone again." Its gaze sharpened on him and he drew back involuntarily at the sight of its teeth. "Alone, till you. Little prince, little hawthorn boy, talked to me in my tree and brought me back into the world. So sweet, so alive."

"Was it just because I called you my friend? There was no other reason that you chose me to be your door?"

"Good friend," the creature reassured him. "Good friend, and true. Kept your promise, at long last."

Loxley swallowed. "And the human child whom you replaced? The Cobb baby?"

The creature dismissed the question with a sharp twitch of one long hand. "Too long ago. Dead now. Away to Faerie in my place to pay the tithe, dead and gone, dead and gone, like all the others. Bones for soil." It tipped its head to one side, regarding him curiously with bright eyes. "And now? For you? England gone, body gone—where do you go in fair summer faelands?"

A breeze whispered through Loxley's curls, warmer than it should have been.

"I need to find Thorncress. Do you know where he is?"

The creature shrugged. "The dead wander as they will. Time stretches, here: find him or not. Have eternity to do."

Loxley's mind shied away from the prospect of eternity. The mere thought of it was disconcerting. And to spend eternity alone . . .

The creature shimmered and flickered, that other form showing through again for a second. "Do what you like. You opened my door; I brought you through. No debt, no favours. Enjoy your summer, little prince. Flower boy, honey child."

It was beside him suddenly, though he hadn't seen it move. Before he could react, it leaned in to place a searing kiss to his mouth, and this time it wasn't cold but the warm, breathing body of a living being, however alien. He kissed back reflexively and it grinned against his lips, nipping at them once—just enough to sting—and then it was gone.

Loxley stood alone in the heather as the sun climbed higher in the fierce blue sky. It seemed as if everything in this world had been embellished and oversaturated. Like the veil had been torn away, or rather, he had pushed through it. The sun warmed his face and slowly melted away the hollow feeling in his bones. Somewhere in Faerie, Thorncress wandered, and Loxley would find him. He chose a direction and began to walk.

As he walked, the land around him changed, and what he saw did not correlate to what he physically felt. Though he still saw solid ground beneath his feet, it seemed to shift around him, so that he sank up to his knees in lush, rolling hills of dense moss. And though he felt only the slightest breeze, the sky shimmered and shone with swiftly-moving patterns like oil on water, with all the colours of a sunset, though he had been convinced it was dawn when he woke. Trees rose up between one moment and the next, glimmering like a mirage before not-quite solidifying, their bark chalky white and blinking at him with dark eyes, like aspens, before turning to glass. They seemed to follow him, the same trees appearing again and again, though he couldn't say how he knew they were the same. Their markings were different, but their wide, staring eyes seemed familiar.

The further on Loxley walked, the less English his surroundings grew, though they were still recognizable as trees and hills and sky. Perhaps, when he was deep enough in Faerie, the landscape would have no physical form at all, and his mind would learn to navigate an entirely new plane of existence. For that was what Faerie was, he felt with increasing certainty: a land no mortal man could truly comprehend.

But for now, the trees remained, and Loxley picked his way across the ground that rolled like the ocean, billowing up around him. One moment he seemed to be wading through waist-high grass, and the next, sinking into thick moss. The glass trees edged closer, almond-shaped eyes gazing out at him from where they hung suspended as if in water inside translucent trunks.

"Did you see a man pass through here some twenty-four hours back?" Loxley asked. "He would have been tall and dark . . . He was looking for someone, too."

The trees gave no answer, but their leaves shivered blue and green in the sunlight. Something that looked not quite like a bird flitted down to perch on his shoulder. It weighed nothing, and gossamer insect wings lay folded against its back. It blinked at Loxley from glass-bright eyes.

"Do you know where he is?" Loxley asked.

Tilting its head to one side, the bird launched itself back into the air with a whir, its wings grazing Loxley's cheek as it passed. It flashed into the sky, where it dove in and out of the strange clouds like a fish dipping through a river. For lack of any better direction, Loxley followed it. He kept his gaze trained on it as he walked, yet he didn't grow dizzy as he normally would, when walking and looking at the sky. Instead, the sky seemed to slip lower until it was all around him, and the layers of clouds became hills and mountains, pink and blue and gold, and he could look through the sky to the place where the atmosphere thinned, and beyond it, into the galaxies themselves.

The stars danced and spun, turning pirouettes and cartwheels, flashing like fireworks before raining down to cling as dewdrops to his eyelashes. Yet, when he stretched his hands above his head, they receded, dancing teasingly just beyond his reach.

He stayed there until time lost all meaning, and thoughts of England gradually slipped from his mind like the last images of a dream. He hadn't always been in Faerie, chasing the stars. He had been looking for someone, or someone had been looking for him, though to what end, he couldn't say. The stars laughed at him in voices like silver bells, spinning out of reach, as the world sighed and rolled around him.

CHAPTER THIRTEEN

THE STRANGER ON THE HILL

The man who had once been called Loxley wandered the crest of a great hill, following the clouds. He did not think of himself as having a name anymore, but then, he didn't think of himself as being a man anymore, either. Such distinctions had long since fallen from his mind. He had a body, but one to which he gave increasingly little thought, beyond how it could move him from one place to another. He suspected that he could move without any body at all, though he had not yet put it to the test.

There was little company to be found in Faerie. Insects sometimes flitted by, like little scraps of paper caught in the breeze, and he heard birds more often than he saw them. There were fish sometimes in the clouds, some small as minnows and moving like quicksilver, and some giant: huge, ponderous things with scales like dragons that twisted and turned in the sky in slow motion. But none of the creatures he saw offered much in the way of conversation. If he had ever been lonely, he no longer remembered. The land around him was company enough.

A white figure flickered in the valley between his hill and the next: a thin, wavering shape like a pale flame. He gazed down at it, studying it until he could make sense of its form. Four legs and a tail like a banner, hound-shaped. It raised its head, catching his scent or perhaps simply so attuned to its surroundings that it had always known he was there, and stared up at him with pale, luminescent green eyes. He stared back, more curious than enthralled, and the hound-shaped being waited as he slowly picked his way down the side of his hill towards it.

When it was certain of his approach, the beast turned and loped up the next hill, ascending without effort. He, on the other hand, still had the muscle memory of his human body, of gravity and the ache of a physical task, and moved slower. The hound paused every few yards, looking back over its shoulder, waiting for him to catch up before coursing on.

It didn't occur to him to let the hound go on without him. Though the beast was an unsettling presence in his mind and in his sight, with too much knowledge held in its pale gaze, there was a familiarity between them, like meeting a stranger he had only seen in a dream.

Upon cresting the next hill, the hound paused, waiting patiently as he climbed up behind it, and then allowed him to approach. The being who had once been called Loxley walked slowly, his body straining from the chase, and his mind shying away from the regal white creature that stood before him. The hound was different from the birds and the insects and the fish he had met thus far, swimming amid the clouds. They had all seemed part of the landscape, mere illusions shimmering into being for his entertainment, but the hound—

The hound watched him with uncanny intelligence, unblinking, the breeze ruffling its thick fur as it stood on the mountaintop and waited for him to gather his courage.

He stopped an arm's length away, and they looked at each other in silence for a moment. The hound's gaze was cool and calm, its ears pricked forward and its tail waving gently back and forth, not in greeting but in simple acknowledgement.

"Do you know me?" asked the being who had once been called Loxley.

He stepped forward, one hand outstretched, but his fingers curled back towards his palm. It wasn't right to touch such a beast as if it were a common dog. Its eyes contained oceans, entire galaxies, and in that instant, he realized that it was as old as the earth itself, some ancient and unknowable being carved from the fabric of the universe.

"Do I know you?" he whispered.

The hound said something in a silvery, musical voice, in a language he couldn't understand. The world shifted on its axis and the ground rumbled under his feet. The hound's tone lilted up, as if in a question, and he shook his head helplessly.

"I don't know what you mean."

The hound padded up to him, closing the space between them in a single step, and pressed its muzzle against his shaking hand. Its nose was cold and wet, its whiskers delicate against his skin, and a flash of recognition passed through him and out the other side. He wanted to bury his hands in its thick fur, to kneel on the ground and beg it to sing for him, to follow it forever, through endless hills and valleys, just to hear its voice again.

But the hound turned away from him, gazing into the next valley where two of its brethren waited: ghostly, canine shapes amid the bright swaths of land. It loped down to them, its long legs making the journey effortless, and only when they were a pack did it glance back up. He stared, his heart in his throat, as three pairs of foxfire eyes met his, before the hounds turned and ran off into the mist. As the clouds swallowed them, they raised their voices to the sky in bright, wild song that echoed through the valley long after they disappeared.

A single tear rolled down his face, burning a trail in its wake. He wiped it away absently, unable to recognize the emotion that birthed it. He had not felt anything but contentment and an appreciation of the strange beauty around him in a very long time.

When he next raised his gaze, there was a new figure standing against the horizon. The stranger stood on the highest peak of a hill like the one where he himself was situated, with a great number more between them, lit from behind so all his features were lost to shadow. A spark of familiarity tugged in the chest of the being who had once been called Loxley, and he frowned. He hadn't seen another person in so long—

The stranger stared at him from across the hills, and, after a moment of returning that stare, the being who was once a man called Loxley walked to meet him. The stranger waited, seemingly content to stand on the peak of his hill like the lord of a mountain, surrounded by wisps of cloud, and lit up by the liquid gold of the sun.

The being who had once been Loxley didn't rush to meet the stranger. Their meeting was inevitable, and whether he ran across the hills or picked his way over them at his leisure made no difference. The stranger would wait. The air was charged, trembling like on the brink of a storm, turning from pink and gold to blue and violet and green, streaked with ribbons of colour like stained glass. The stranger watched him patiently as he climbed the last hill between them, stopping only when they were a yard apart.

The stranger was familiar. The being who had once been Loxley had seen his face in a dream, perhaps. His hair was long, falling in dark waves over his shoulders, with sepia skin and coal-dark eyes. They were warm eyes, ringed with sooty lashes so dark that they almost disguised the heavy circles under them.

"I know you," said the being who was once Loxley. Frowning, he closed the space between them and took the stranger's hand. For a second, he expected to find the skin cold, though he couldn't say why—but the stranger's grip was warm and firm. "I know you," he repeated, more confidently.

"And I know you."

"You're the man from the moors . . ."

"And you're the man from the faerie ring."

The being who was once Loxley dropped the stranger's hand and stumbled back as the memories of another life stirred in his breast. He had known nothing but clouds and hills and Faerie for so long that he couldn't recognize the life that presented itself to him from within his mind's eye. He caught a glimpse of too-small beds pulled close to the hearth, leather gloves and heavy coats, and snow blanketing frost-ravaged soil. Had the world ever been so bleak, so grey? He couldn't imagine such cold, not anymore.

He remembered the feel of the stranger's hands on his body, the feel of his lips, of his—

Stepping forward, he caught the stranger's face in both hands and pulled him into a searing kiss. The instant their lips met, he remembered everything: sleet and snow, the dread of what was to come, waking to a cold bed with the body of the man he loved, digging the grave that he may as well have laid down in himself. The bay of the hounds and the terrible, aching loneliness that drove him north again. The hawthorn and the brown-capped mushrooms that marked his final resting place.

Loxley's eyes stung as he pulled back, tears rolling down his cheeks. Thorncress gazed back at him, one hand on Loxley's shoulder, the other in his hair. He was darker than he had been before, the bright Faerie sun tanning him browner than the weak light of England ever could.

"I had hoped I wouldn't find you here." Thorncress' voice was rough from disuse, but it sounded as music to Loxley's ears.

"You left me." Loxley's voice came out cracked and broken. He had spoken to no one but the stars in a long time.

"I'm sorry for it. I didn't mean to."

"You—what?"

"That night," Thorncress said slowly. "In the yard, when you sought to shield me from the hounds, and you begged me to stay—I would have given anything to do as you wished. But it was too late. I had already seen them from the window, two days prior. Before you burned your hawthorn apple."

Loxley stared at him, trying to rebuild his memories of that time. "You never told me. I thought you safe."

"I didn't want you tortured by it. What could either of us have done? You stayed with me. That was all I wanted."

"I thought you safe," Loxley repeated.

"Forgive me. I know what it is to be left behind."

Loxley crushed him to his chest, wrapping him in as firm an embrace as he could, and Thorncress collapsed into him with a sigh of relief.

"You have my coat," he murmured.

"I wanted to keep something of you with me." Loxley brushed his tears aside. "So, you kept your promise, however unintentionally. Did you find your Rosa?"

Thorncress' expression shuttered. "She doesn't remember me. She doesn't even remember herself."

"But you found her."

"I did." Thorncress passed a hand over his face, raking his hair back from his temples. "Though I can't say what it was I found. Not a sister, in any case. Perhaps not even a human soul, not after all this time."

Loxley hesitated before drawing out the letter in its worn envelope. "I read it, after you were gone. I wanted to understand."

"Did it help?"

"No."

Thorncress touched the letter without taking it, tracing the tattered remains of the seal. "You should have buried it with me. I should have buried it with her."

"I'm sorry."

"As am I." Thorncress offered him a tired smile. "I should never have expected more. But she seems happy."

"And you?" Loxley asked tentatively. "Do you consider your oath fulfilled?"

"To her, yes. To you . . ."

Loxley kissed him quickly, before any more self-recriminations could fall from his lips. "All our time together was merely postponing the inevitable," he said firmly, when they parted. "I was doomed from the moment I told that creature my name at four years old. You made the waiting more endurable, and for that, I'm grateful." He linked their fingers. "And now that I've found you again, all is well."

"Could you fend the creature off without me?"

Loxley paused, and Thorncress seemed to read the truth in his eyes, for he heaved a sigh and shook his head.

"Did you even try?"

"I gave myself to it," Loxley admitted, resolutely refusing to feel any shame. "I crossed over on the following dawn. One day after you—after you died. How long have you been here?"

Thorncress' brow furrowed. "Years, I should think. I recall little of England, as a whole. I remember you now, and us together, but . . ." He shrugged, his gaze dropping to their joined hands. "I had forgotten myself, before you found me. I thought there was little point in clinging to my old life, after finding Rosa. She didn't cling to hers, after all."

"And you didn't expect me to follow you over."

"I'd hoped you wouldn't."

Loxley lifted their hands to kiss his knuckles. "I couldn't bear leaving you in the ground. My last memory of you was in that lonely grave, with the black earth piling in all around."

"I'm sorry."

Loxley shook the memories away. "No matter. I've found you, and you won't leave me behind again so easily. So, now that we're both in Faerie: what do we do?"

Rolling his shoulders, Thorncress gazed out over the hills, painted in stripes of green and blue and pink. "I don't know the way back. I'm not sure there is one. We are dead, after all."

"The Fair Folk pass between worlds often enough." Loxley couldn't bring himself to be particularly troubled, not when he had Thorncress' hand in his again. "If there is a way, we'll happen upon it eventually."

"I suppose we will."

"The creature was right about the weather, at least. There's not the slightest chill to the air. I don't miss being damp."

Thorncress glanced at him. "Is that your way of saying that you don't overly mind having to stay?"

Loxley shrugged. Faerie was beautiful, enchantingly so, and with that beauty came the sweet, honeyed urge to leave the last trappings of England behind. "I suppose if we stay long enough, we'll forget our world and ourselves entirely, as Rosa did."

"It's likely," Thorncress said thoughtfully, gazing out over the hilltops. "I don't know if that's such a terrible thing. There's little in England for me to miss."

Loxley would miss the comfort of a fire in the hearth, and the sight of freshly fallen snow glittering in the yard at night when all was still and silent, and the delicate beauty of the year's first frost. But he would not miss the aching cold in his bones, nor the sorrow of losing one whom he loved without having the chance to say goodbye. He had made his choice to follow Thorncress beyond the veil, and he could not regret it. Perhaps someone had found his body, where it lay in its little ring of brown-capped mushrooms, all alone in the northern wilds. Or perhaps no one would ever find him, and the foxes and ravens would speak his only eulogy from between sharp teeth and wicked beaks, consigning him to the earth in their foreign tongues. He found he did not mind the thought.

"With enough time, perhaps we'll turn into trees, and the wind will carry our seeds back to England, where we can start life anew."

Thorncress glanced him. "How romantic."

"It's as good a thought as any."

"True enough. Whatever my form, I'm glad of the company."

Loxley hesitated. "You won't go back to Rosa?"

"She doesn't even know my name. I was chasing a ghost. I should have let her go years ago." Thorncress blew out his breath, tipping his head back to look into the sky. The sun brought out the colours in his hair: strands of gold and auburn buried amid the dark, rich brown, with shots of silver here and there. "But it's over now. It's done."

Squeezing his hand, Loxley leaned in to press a kiss first to Thorncress' jaw, and then his lips. He tasted sweeter than before, like his mouth was full of summer honey, and the perfume of a thousand flowers hung in the air. Loxley didn't care if it was an illusion. Untangling their fingers, he brought his hand to Thorncress' face, drawing him closer to deepen the kiss. They had not kissed enough when they were alive, and he meant to remedy it now that they were dead.

"We shall look for the road home," he murmured against Thorncress' skin, drawing his hands over his shoulders to search out the warm, brown skin hidden by his shirt collar. "If anyone can find it, it will be you. And until then, we'll stay side by side, and if we forget the world, we'll forget it together. And if we turn into trees, we'll grow so near to one another that our roots will tangle under the ground, and we won't be able to tell where one of us ends and the other begins. We'll be together, this time."

"I promise."

The sun was too large and too bright, and the landscape felt alive all around them, but it was their land. As they fell to the ground, the wildflowers grew to cushion them, a gentle embrace as they wrapped around one another. When Thorncress touched him, everything turned to honey and dewdrops and foxgloves, and the heady taste of midsummer wine, and all else washed away in a haze of pleasure.

When he next opened his eyes, his face was pressed to Thorncress' shoulder, and he could scarcely remember why he had ever thought of looking for a way home at all.

"Your burns are gone," Thorncress noted, touching Loxley's throat.

The skin no longer hurt, nor stripped away beneath his fingers. Lifting his right hand, Loxley inspected his index finger, and found that it was pale and smooth, and that the little scar was as it had ever been.

"Is there a bruise?" he asked.

Thorncress drew his thumb down the line of Loxley's neck. "No, nothing."

"How strange this life, that you should finally meet me unenchanted only when we are both in Faerie."

"Strange indeed."

Loxley stretched up to kiss his mouth. He tasted of pollen and honey mead. He tasted nothing of home. Rolling onto his back, Loxley gazed up at the bright sky. England's skies were flat and grey, nothing like this dizzying, ever-shifting array of colour. England was . . .

He reached out blindly for Thorncress' hand and pulled it to his chest. "But we won't forget each other again, will we? Even if we forget everything else?"

"I won't allow it," Thorncress said, and the knot in Loxley's chest loosened.

"I love you." His heart still skipped a beat when he said it aloud: and in broad daylight, too. He would never have dared such a thing back home, but in Faerie, who could judge him for it?

"And I, you."

"You told me once to look for Faerie through the clouds. Perhaps that's our way back. From out amidst the stars."

"There are cities here. And kingdoms with great, glittering courts. Places made of glass and crystal and abalone shell, far more beautiful than your London ever dreamed of being. You should see those, first."

Loxley hummed contentedly. Thorncress was warm and breathing beside him, smelling of cinnamon and orange and bonfire smoke, just as he had the first time they'd met. Where he went, Loxley would follow. The road to England could wait.

ACKNOWLEDGEMENTS

Thanks to K.D., for always answering all my questions; my parents, for supporting my efforts from afar; Neurts, for listening to me announce that "I'm definitely finishing the draft this week," for several months on end, with zero proof of progress; and Grimshaw, with his gentle snoot and his soft, silky ears, whom I was compelled to pat at great length every time after writing a single mention of the hounds. He is far from an awe-inspiring hound of legend, but he'll always be my favourite dog.

ABOUT THE AUTHOR

Arden Powell is an author and illustrator from the Canadian East Coast. A nebulous entity, they live with a small terrier and an exorbitant number of houseplants, and have conversations with both. They write fantasy, romance, horror, and comedy, often in combination, but rarely two consecutive books in the same genre. Everything they write is queer.

They can be found on twitter @ArdenPowell, or follow their blog at ardenpowell.wordpress.com for email updates on upcoming releases and infrequent posts.

Printed in Great Britain
by Amazon